West with Hopeless

Carolyn
Lieberg

DUTTON CHILDREN'S BOOKS

NEW YORK

Library of Congress Cataloging-in-Publication Data

Lieberg, Carolyn S.
    West with Hopeless/Carolyn Lieberg.—1st ed.
        p.   cm.
    Summary: Bound for Reno and their divorced father for the
summer, two half sisters leave from Iowa in an old Ford Escort
and learn a great deal about the people they encounter and
even more about themselves.
    ISBN 0-525-47194-4
    [1. Sisters—Fiction.   2. Automobile travel—Fiction.
3. Divorce—Fiction.]   I. Title.
PZ7. L61629We 2004
[Fic]—dc22   2003019472

Published in the United States by Dutton Children's Books,
a division of Penguin Young Readers Group
345 Hudson Street, New York, New York 10014
www.penguin.com

Printed in USA · Designed by Tim Hall
First Edition
1 3 5 7 9 10 8 6 4 2

WITH LOVE TO RACHEL AND ADRIA

Acknowledgments

I would like especially to thank my editor, Julie Strauss-Gabel, for her kindness, her enthusiasm, and her nurturing advice. I want to express appreciation to my agent, Barry Goldblatt, for cheery and steady support, and to Craig Johnson and Patricia Cone for friendship and patience. Many thanks to my dear writing pals, Delia Ray Howard, Tess Weaver Gullickson, Jennifer Reinhardt, Julia Wasson, and Adeline Hooper-Samuels; to caring friends and family; and to Robin for faithful companionship. Finally, I wish to express profound gratitude to Michael T. Bailey—for the present and for memory; for little, nameless, unremembered acts of kindness and of love.

Heartfelt thanks to the Ragdale Foundation for a two-week block of writing time some years ago, where the seeds of this book, in a far different guise, first appeared.

Tourists don't know where they've been,
travelers don't know where they're going.

— PAUL THEROUX

West with Hopeless

1

Ever since my folks split—when I was seven—I've lived with my mom in Davenport, Iowa, and until right now, I've always gone west for the summer on an airplane. This time, I just learned, I was going in a car with my sister, make that *half sister*. Hope.

"How soon?"

Mom put her hand on my shoulder. "Tomorrow, I'm afraid."

"Tomorrow!?! That's impossible! I can't." Getting mad was useless, but I couldn't help it. If there was one thing I hated most about being a kid, it was this very thing. I'd make plans, and then in a single minute they could be changed by someone.

She looked down for a minute. "Look at it this way, Carin. You'll be there in less than a week. Your summer will get rolling that much sooner."

I plopped down on my bed. "I barely have time to pack. This is so unfair. It's so *sudden*."

Mom ignored my words. *Ignored* them. Even though my parents got along, which I was grateful for, since lots of divorced parents are horrid to each other, sometimes I wanted one of them to be mad, to take *my* side. Like now.

"Your dad has wired Hope three hundred dollars for motels and food. She needs to be in Reno by Saturday for this job interview your father has arranged."

I bit my lower lip. Tuesday, Wednesday, Thursday, Friday, Saturday—five days in a car with Hope. Yuk. She was pretty much everything you don't want in a sister—selfish, bossy, crabby. I loved her, of course, but I didn't always like her much. How we both happened to have the same dad or to have lived in the same house for seven years was astonishing as far as I was concerned. And I was pretty sure she felt the same way. Dad seemed to pretend it was just a phase—for *both* of us. He always acted as if we were about to become best friends. Dreamer.

"An interview? She's leaving Chicago?"

Mom nodded. "You know, Carin, you might end up having some fun. Maybe this'll be a real adventure."

"An adventure?" I said. My forehead felt wrinkled up, and I hoped I wouldn't cry.

"There you'll be, cruising across America, strangers to the left of you, strangers to the right of you. Sounds like an adventure to me."

"And the *strangerest* one will be behind the wheel. Very funny, Mom."

She reached around my shoulder and hugged me. "That's me, Mrs. Funny. You're pretty funny yourself."

"But tomorrow?" I said in a small voice. I didn't *want* to go yet. It wasn't time.

4

"I am sorry, Carin." She held me tightly. "Sometimes there are circumstances beyond our control."

"I can't even call Jenna to let her know." My best friend was off for two weeks at her grandparents' place in Kentucky. I wouldn't see her until August anyway, but I wished I could tell her about this change.

Mom pulled back and took my hands in hers. "You can e-mail her from Dad's once she's home—or even write her a letter."

I looked at Mom, and her face opened into a grin. She was trying to make me feel better, so I tried harder. "Come on," she urged. "It really might be fine, you know. You girls used to sing and play car games, remember? You actually had fun sometimes." Mom's smile faded. "Carin, don't scowl."

"Sorry. I'll be OK." In truth, I wanted to sink deeply into a good long session of self-pity—hang my head, kick walls, and scream.

Mom planted a loud kiss on the end of my nose. "We've got lots to do. You pack and I'll see about laundry. Then groceries."

I smiled at her, because I didn't really want to be mad. Not at Mom.

When she left, I popped in an old Aretha Franklin tape for comfort, and started pulling clothes out of my drawers. During my summers in Reno, one of the things I missed about my room in Iowa were the maps, a giant one of the United States and another really old one that showed the local area before Iowa was even a state.

I stopped sorting clothes and stepped over to the big map, putting the tip of my finger on Davenport—right on the Mississippi River. I dragged a path across Iowa, Nebraska, Wyoming, Utah, and Nevada, all the way to Reno, where my dad taught photography. Unbelievable. Could this trip actually work? I shook my head and returned to my clothes.

Mom bought the other map at a yard sale. It was titled IOWA TERRITORY—1838. I liked how old it looked and all the things that it didn't show. A few towns dotted the land, and a few counties hugged the Mississippi. My county, Scott, was pink. Other counties were green and blue. Beyond the counties the map was all deep yellow with no lines at all, just the words *Neutral Ground*. It wasn't really neutral, of course. Tribes lived there. I often wondered what the mapmaker thought when he wrote *Neutral Ground*. Now most of it was Iowa, orderly with fields and roads—just one part of the land that Hope and I would cross on our way west.

The other things I missed when I was at Dad's were the photos on my dresser. Most of the pictures were of my best friend, Jenna, and me—dressed up for holiday plays for the neighborhood, hunched over in the silly spy costumes we made in the third grade, and standing in frosting-splotched aprons next to the tilting tower cake we baked two years ago for her mom's birthday. In a bigger frame, Dad and I balanced on Rollerblades with the Rocky Mountains all grand behind us. The final photo was from last fall's trip down the Wapsie River with Mom. There we were, giggling and shivering, perched in a canoe in our swimsuit tops and cutoffs. We'd tipped over not three minutes earlier, and our hair was still sopping wet. I love the way pictures pull you back into a time that's gone and remind you of all the things that don't show in the photo.

"Carin," Mom called from downstairs. "I'm heading to the store. I'll try to be quick."

It was dusk when I heard Mom's car pull up behind the house. When I looked out my window, I could see why. She opened the trunk, and I looked down on bags and bags of groceries; it seemed like more food than I'd ever seen her buy at one time.

After a few minutes, she came upstairs with a basket of clean laundry and plopped it on the floor. "When you're done packing, come on down."

I put some of the clothes into my drawers and finished filling my gym bag and two boxes to ship to Reno. This was my custom, for good reason. When I was four, we drove to Canada. Dad had a photography project—a calendar of waterbirds. He took enough photos for a *five*-year calendar, but on the way home, driving along a winding river, he spotted a rare tern in the distance and pulled over to photograph it. He headed off quietly, his camera lens leading the way. Not knowing how long he'd be gone, the rest of us piled out of the car noiselessly, as we'd been taught, leaving the doors open.

As we stood around carefully not talking, company arrived. A skunk. It strolled out of the woods, eyed us as if we were old friends, and marched right between Hope and me. We looked at each other wide-eyed and froze. Then the skunk hopped into the car, and I couldn't help it. I screamed. That did it. Mom and Hope screamed, too. The skunk did what skunks do, then sprang out of the car, and hightailed it back into the woods.

Dad ran back to us, and we drove all the way from Canada to Davenport in one long race for clean air, the windows open and the wind whipping through the car. Whenever we had to slow down, we were trapped in skunk fog.

For weeks afterward, we'd go to the Hy-Vee Grocery and buy cans of tomato juice to wash the inside of the car and everything that had been "skunked." My favorite stuffed animal had been a white duck, which, thanks to the tomato juice, became forever pink.

I vowed never again to travel with all of my things.

Remembering "skunk summer" reminded me of other car trips. Hope and I always fought for territory. We both had stuff under our feet, and it made us scrappy. One time Dad put a piece of duct tape all the way down the seat from the back window to the floor. It helped, but it didn't stop us. The truth was that neither of us wanted to share the backseat. Now we were going to have to share a front seat for five days.

I took a deep breath to push those memories out of the way and carried my gym bag downstairs. I could hear Mom in the kitchen. When I walked in, the scene made me smile. There was a cloth on the table, the lights were off, and candles were burning. Steam rose from two cups, each filled to the brim, capped by islands of marshmallows that looked like a gathering of baby seals.

I sat down. Mom stirred her cup of cocoa. "A little quiet moment before you leave."

I dipped my spoon in and heard a dull clunk when it hit the peppermint candy, melting and spicing the cocoa. As I stirred, the marshmallows melted and I slurped a spoonful.

"Mom, do you think three hundred dollars will be enough to get us halfway across the country? It seems like a lot of money to me, but . . ."

"It'll be fine if you do things like buy some of your meals at grocery stores instead of restaurants."

"If Hope uses her brain."

"She *is* an adult, remember."

"Technically, anyway."

"And you'll find plenty of budget places to sleep if you avoid the big cities. I'll give you some extra money. Just in case." She gave me a quick smile and added, "In case something goes wrong with the car. It's not the newest thing on the road."

I repeated her excuse in my mind: *In case something goes wrong with the car.* Just hearing her say it aloud seemed like a temptation for fate.

Mom suddenly handed me a small package wrapped in the Sunday comics section. "Here—a going-away gift."

I pulled the paper off and lifted the lid. Inside was a compass on a long green cord. "This is beautiful." I put it around my neck. "With Hope driving, it'll be extra handy. Thanks."

Mom laughed. "I bought you a phone card, too. I hope you'll check in a couple of times, so your poor mum knows where you are." She made a little *missing-you-already* smile and quickly nodded to the wall behind me, where she had tacked a map of the United States—a smaller one than I had in my room.

"Doesn't Hope have a cell phone?"

"I don't know. But you'll have the card anyway."

The Kit Kat Klock struck nine, and the other clocks on the wall clicked in near unison to the ninth hour, all of their hands making perfect right angles. Mom'd been buying clocks at garage sales for a long time. A few years ago, she stopped trying to decide which one to use, and just put all nineteen up, which made the wall seem alive. She liked the way they were busy all the time. I liked how they seemed like company, but soon I'd be gone, and they would tick on without me.

"Hey, I almost forgot. Grams sent a box of candy for you again this year."

"A Whitman's Sampler?" I actually didn't like all the chocolates, but I liked the chart in the top that told you what they had inside. And I liked the hard yellow boxes— always good for something. "That was nice of her."

"Call her when you get to Reno." Mom drew her thumbnail along the design of her cup. Suddenly she stood up. "Well, let's finish up. It's getting late."

I took my dishes to the sink. As I turned to go upstairs,

I noticed the nail over the sink where we kept dried wishbones. Five or six of them straddled the nail, looking like dancers' legs in a difficult stretch. Our house rule was that you could take one of the wishbones whenever you needed a little boost. I lifted one off the nail and went upstairs. As I slipped it into a small zippered pocket in my backpack, I remembered the way Hope and I always broke them for wishes when we were younger.

"Here, Carin," she'd say in her *I've-got-you-now* voice. She'd hold out the wishbone, and I'd grab it, certain that for once it would break on her side of the knob, and I'd get *my* wish after all. "Ready?"

I'd close my eyes and make a very serious wish. I didn't believe in throwing away even the smallest chance for a wish to come true.

Snap! "I won!" Hope would whoop. Always. And when she won, it seemed she wasn't happy just to have her wish. She was also happy about beating me, about proving that she was smarter, wiser, luckier. It seemed like she had to win, no matter what we were doing. The last time we broke a wishbone, I saw how near the knob she held her side. When I accused her of cheating, she yelled that I was a whiner and a sore loser.

I liked the way Mom and I used the wishbones much better.

That night I slept in Mom's bed, as I always did before my trips to Reno. She fell asleep first. When her breath sounded regular and deep, I turned toward her, slipped my fingers under the sleeve of her T-shirt, and gripped the hem. Her arm felt warm on the back of my hand. I held on.

When it came down to this night, this last night every year, I felt torn about walking away from my Iowa life. I wanted terribly to see Dad, because I missed him so much and I loved our summers together, but I didn't want to leave Mom. I didn't want to leave this home.

2

It was after eleven when I heard a car pull in behind the house. Hope's old Ford Escort was just like Jenna's mom's, except Hope's was an ugly copper color. It reminded me of a piece of cheap carnival jewelry with a crust of rust.

I'd spent the morning rearranging my backpack with the Whitman Sampler candy box and lots of travel basics like paper, pens, scissors, tape, a small atlas, a big map of Iowa, lots of gum, and other stuff to fill the many travel hours that would now be my Tuesday, Wednesday, Thursday, Friday, and Saturday. I'd also changed clothes a few times, finally settling on a white T-shirt and pale blue shorts, and of course, my compass. Mom wound my dark straight hair into a tight French braid, though I knew that by the end of the day, it would be half-braid, half-wind knots.

I was trying not to dread this trip. I knew I should be mature about it. I was determined to try my best.

Looking through the window, I could see that Hope had turned off the engine but was just sitting there, window down, her elbow resting on the chrome strip. I went out.

"Howdy," she said.

"Howdy?"

"Check out the sign." She nodded to the backseat window on her side. Taped to the inside was a sign that said WESTWARD HO! in bold, black letters with a lot of colorful curlicue artwork for a border.

"Who did that?"

"A friend."

I looked around the sign into the backseat; it was a jumble of floppy plastic baskets and some shopping bags. It didn't look anything like the way Mom and Dad had packed when we went on trips.

"Ready to go?" Hope stepped out of the car and tugged the tail of my braid. I hated that. And I was even two inches taller than she was.

"Yes." I nearly said, *Ready and waiting,* but I didn't.

Hope's black, black eyebrows and turtle-green eyes reminded me of things in tanks at Paws and Claws. Her short reddish hair was always a snarl, even when she claimed that it was a style—it always looked like part of some experiment to me. Her skin wasn't quite as bad as it used to be.

"Hi, Hope," Mom called from the back door. "How was your trip? Come on in, you two, and get the food."

"Hi," Hope called back as we walked to the house. They hugged each other. "I see the wall is still ticking away," Hope said, motioning to the clocks. "Traffic out of Chicago was easy, for a change."

Mom smiled. "Here are your treats." She pointed to a plastic cooler with cheese singles, fruit, and cans of soda and sparkling water. Next to it was a paper sack with mini cans of tuna, crackers, bananas, rice cakes, and chips, corn *and* potato.

Hope looked at the cooler and at the bag. "We could get to L.A. on this."

"L.A.—ha," Mom said. "The way you two eat on the road? From my memory, I'd say if it gets you to Des Moines, you're lucky."

"Let's go," I said, pulling my backpack onto one shoulder and grabbing my gym bag. Hope grunted as she lifted the cooler. When I heard the screen door bounce shut behind us, the sound gave me a little twinge of homesickness. Already.

"How will this food fit in the backseat with all your stuff there?" I snapped as we headed to her car.

"It's a hatchback. There's plenty of room. *Just relax,*" she snapped back. She set the cooler down, opened her door, and flipped the driver's seat forward. Then she began pulling out her flimsy containers like a dog going after a bone.

Just relax. Her voice echoed in my head. Ugh.

Mom peered into the car. "Hey, I forgot it was an Escort," she joked. "Just what you girls need, huh? Get it?" She forced a little laugh and nodded to the WESTWARD HO! "Cute sign."

"A friend made it," Hope said.

"I bet you girls'll be halfway across Nebraska before nightfall," Mom said cheerfully.

Hope's voice was muffled inside the back of the car. "Carin, where's your stuff?"

I handed her the small gym bag. "Mom's shipping the rest."

Hope nodded. "Oh, yeah. Skunks."

"I also bought a bag of ice," Mom said. "I'll get it." We always took ice on trips: cubes for chewing on or cooling our sweaty skin. And, of course, Hope and I used to have fights, dropping them down each other's shirts.

Hope pulled the hatchback closed. "Time for the cooler." She lifted it, aimed it toward the backseat, and lunged forward. The cooler promptly got wedged between the door frame and the edge of the seat.

"Help me, will you?" she said.

I pulled the passenger seat up and slid into the back. Hope leaned on the cooler again.

"You need to lift it more," I said.

She lifted a little and pushed again. We were trying to get a big straight thing to go around a corner, and whatever we did seemed to get us nowhere.

"*You* lift while I shove," she said.

So I lifted, she shoved, and suddenly the thing plopped onto the seat, where it would probably stay until we reached Reno.

"We did it," I said.

I was afraid this maneuver was a sample of how the trip would go. Hope would push when she should have been lifting, and I would yank when there was nothing free to pull. If we were lucky, things would pop into place. If not, then what? Disaster?

When I looked up, Mom was standing by the front

bumper, the bag of ice hanging from one fist. Hope was by the driver's door, one foot on the frame, and I stood at the passenger side. We three were the points of an isosceles triangle, I thought, it being one of the last things I'd learned about in math this year. We stood still, as though held to the moment, pinned to the uneven safety of family habits. But I couldn't resist thinking about Mom keeping the point firmly in place while Hope and I drove away, pulling two sides of this triangle with us, mile after mile.

Hope and I stepped into the car. I knew Mom hated the good-byes, but since it happened every year, we were growing used to it. She was the one who always said that there's no way to stop time. No matter what was coming, it was best to get on with it, get into it, and get it over with.

Mom looked up toward the summer sun and lifted the ice bag a little. "I hope this lasts a while; it's going to be hot." She walked to Hope's side and gave her a hug as she flopped the bag between the seats. "Take care now."

"We will," Hope said.

Then she came to my side and kissed and hugged me tight. She smelled like her perfume and her shampoo and coffee and toothpaste. I breathed her in for the last time till the end of summer. She pulled out a little packet of Kleenex from her pocket. "Tuck this in your backpack. You might need it." She moved to the front of the car again. "Now get out of here. You've got some miles to cover."

We buckled our seat belts. Hope twisted the key and the engine started right up. "What's the mileage, if I may ask."

17

She looked through the steering wheel at the row of numbers. "One two six five five five."

I wrote down 126,555 in my notebook, where I'd already written:

Latitude—41° 32' N
Longitude—90° 28' W

In school we had to learn about the degrees and minutes mapmakers use in geography and of course had to memorize Davenport's.

Distance from Davenport—0 miles
Distance to Reno—1,763 miles

I'd added up the miles last night. The number was so big.

"Thanks. Let's go."

So far, so good.

As we backed out of the driveway, I glanced at my compass. We were heading west, down the alley. It was only the beginning of west, but it was a start.

3

She flipped on the radio and bopped her head to the staticky music while her fingertips drummed on the steering wheel. "Crappy radio and no AC," she said. "There's a tape player, but it's broken, too."

What a relief. Who knew *what* we'd have had to listen to.

Hope's auburn hair looked like it often did—sticking out in strange directions, as though she'd applied a lot of mousse and then used a broken vacuum. It looked very unplanned. And her clothes, too. Two or maybe three— depending upon whether or not she was wearing a bra— tank tops, their thin straps spread over her shoulder like guitar strings, and purple velveteen shorts. Mom said her style was the effect of going to a fashion school, but if you asked me it looked more like a *side* effect. She wore hefty round hoops in her ears, plus an extra stud at the top of one, and a gold necklace with three jade stones that had been her mom's. I couldn't remember ever seeing her without the necklace.

"So what are the food groups back there?" she asked with what seemed like excessive good cheer.

"You're hungry already?"

"No breakfast here, Sis," she said. "And I've already been on the road for three hours."

I hated being called *Sis,* but I let it go. "She told us in the kitchen. Rice cakes and stuff. Grapes for you. And apples."

"Apples, of course. Cathy food. I'd like one."

Not a mile from home, and I was already being bossed around.

The tissue packet from Mom was still clamped in my fist. I tugged one out before shoving the pack into my back-pack. Then I undid my seat belt so I could climb around and dig into the cooler.

We headed down Brady Street toward the interstate. On the entrance ramp stood a barefoot guy in ripped-off pants and a dirty baseball cap. His thumb was high in the air. Next to him were a huge, grimy duffel bag and a small, dirty dog that might have been a Pekinese. Both of them looked to be in serious need of a bath. If you want a free ride, I think the least you can do is try to clean up a little. Maybe even put a ribbon in the Pekinese's hair.

As the car rounded the cloverleaf and pulled onto the freeway, I blinked hard and looked back at Davenport as best I could around Hope's profile and the WESTWARD HO! sign. I couldn't keep a lump from growing in my throat.

I imagined Mom still in the yard, standing as she had been when we drove away, staring at the place where the car had been. I was clutched with panic as I thought of all the miles Hope and I would travel and how easy it would be to get lost and how there would be no finding my way back. I tried to push the thought away, and twisted farther in my seat to watch the highway grow long and skinny behind us. I made myself remember that it was hard and deep, too. No matter what happened, that path of asphalt would always lead back to Davenport. The idea calmed me. Nevertheless I reached for my hairbrush, unwound a single strand from between the bristles, and tossed it out the window to leave a small piece of me behind. Call me superstitious, I don't care.

I pulled out the Iowa map and found the Mississippi, Davenport, and names of familiar towns across the state—Iowa City, Grinnell, Pella. I touched each word and checked my compass again for *west* before I refolded it.

What a long way we had to go. Five days with Hope in charge.

We sped on, Hope chomping the apple, one hand on the wheel, weaving around semis like we were on a theme-park ride.

"Could you drive like a grown-up, please?"

She ignored me. I opened my backpack and reached for a ziplock bag. This one held embroidery floss, a pair of small scissors, large safety pins, and a round metal case not much bigger than a LifeSaver where a yard-long measuring tape was coiled. I pulled out a big safety pin with dangling threads. I was weaving a bracelet for Jenna.

In the winter, I worked on the woven bracelets by pinning the safety pin to my jeans. In the summer, I used an invention I made myself by attaching the safety pin to an old tennis wristband of Dad's. I slid the elastic band over my foot and up to my knee.

With my feet planted on the dashboard, I began cross-ing the threads and pulling them tight. I had to admit the small car was the perfect size for this project. I felt a little rush of happiness, because something was going well.

Hope glanced at the woven strip. "Still doing those?"

I nodded.

Years earlier, it was Hope who'd taught me how to make them, the four-thread kind. Then, on my own, I'd figured out some complicated patterns, and now I used six or eight strands. "Hey, you've got the designs going both ways." She sounded impressed. "And you've got more threads. Cool."

I nodded and couldn't keep a small smile of pride off my face.

We drove on a while, with the bad radio, rushing wind, and the droning noise of tires on pavement. A pickup truck passed us with squares of sod piled high. They reminded me of the stacks of carpet samples at the entrance to the grocery store.

After Hope'd nipped off the last bite of apple, she hand-ed me the core. "Here."

I looked up from my work. "Yeah?"

"Take it," she snapped, giving me an irritated glance. "Passengers are in charge of trash." Then she dropped it in my lap.

"Yuk. Why don't you throw it out?"

"I don't want to. Isn't that good enough?"

"Whatever happened to *please* and *thank you?*"

"Please and thank you," she said sarcastically. "Do you want to argue all the way to Nevada?"

I didn't want to argue, in fact, and her question reminded me that this trip was supposed to be an adventure. *Have some fun*, Mom had said. Right. OK.

Instead of tossing the apple in the trash bag, I took out my roll of Scotch tape, held the core to the back of the rearview mirror so the bottom half was in view, and taped it up.

"A shrine to dead food?"

"Our first souvenir." Part of the flesh was already darkening.

She smiled and put both hands on the steering wheel, which made me feel safer.

"Look," Hope said, pointing off to the right. "Wacky Waters."

I watched the kids roaring down the high wet slide toward the huge pool. "Mom and I were *supposed* to go Saturday," I said, sulking.

"Look, your complaining is getting old real fast. If you want me to, I can pull over and you can call Dad and tell *him* how ticked off you are. It's not my fault."

"I know. I'm sorry." I said it quietly because I only half wanted her to hear me over the car noise. I had to try to be pleasant, even if it was pretend. I went back to my bracelet to get away from the spiky air.

When I sneaked a look at Hope, she seemed to be concentrating hard on the road and fingering her necklace, which she did a lot. Maybe it was time for a peace offering. I pulled out the candy box from Grandma. "Want a chocolate?"

She glanced over. "A Whitman's Sampler. Cool. What's there?"

I read from the chart in the lid: "Butter Cream Caramel, Almonds, Coconut Cream, Vermont Fudge—"

"Vermont Fudge sounds just right."

I handed her the chocolate, took one myself, and placed the box under my seat, trying not to juggle the candies out of order.

"Where'd you get that?"

"Grandma. She sent one last year, too."

"It seems like Whitman's Samplers have been around forever," Hope said.

"Really?"

Hope shrugged. "Not quite, but I bet they've been around since Grandma was young. I guess that's not quite forever, is it, but it's *her* forever. You know?"

I guess I looked puzzled.

"Like . . . like color film for us instead of only black and white."

I stared off above the fields, my gaze catching on the clusters of trees that marked farmsteads. "It seems like color film has always been around."

"Yeah, well, everything that was here when you were born has been around for your *own* forever. You take it for granted. Like Walkmans or plastic shoes."

Suddenly Hope gasped and a truck's shadow rushed over us, its air horn blasting us out of our seats. Hope shouted. The semi blazed ahead, leaning and weaving close to cars and other trucks as it barreled down the hill.

"Man!" Hope said.

"Think his brakes went?" I asked, a little shaky.

"Who knows? At least he's getting far away from us."

She straightened up behind the wheel and drove on. I returned to my threads. Blue over green, tie with black. Pink under. Pull tight. Press flat. Each color with a beginning and an ending, on its own predictable path.

Before long, the car began to slow. I looked up to find we were pulling off the freeway. "What's wrong?" I asked. "Where are we?"

"Iowa City. I've got to do a couple things." She scratched her thigh with a long fingernail and pulled up to the stop sign.

I shrank down in my seat. After a few stoplights, she pulled into the parking lot of a Laundromat.

"What's going on," I demanded.

Hope rolled her eyes.

"Jeez, I just asked. You drag me around like I'm some old blanket. You could tell me why we're here, you know. It's pretty annoying that we're supposed to be driving to Nevada, and you're already stopping the car."

She turned to me and slowly formed the words: "I. Need. To. Wash. Some. Clothes."

"Why didn't you wash them before you left?"

"I didn't have time."

I slapped my hands on the dashboard in disgust.

Hope narrowed her eyes at me. "I don't need this."

Like I do?

The Laundromat sat between a bagel place and a small

25

cement-block building with no windows that had a religious sign welcoming one and all. Buildings without windows give me the creeps; you never know what's inside.

Hope pulled a grocery bag off the heap in back, and I followed her into the Laundromat. The place was hotter inside than out because of the dryers. Taped to a bulletin board was a crayoned sign that read, SORRY. AC BROKEN.

Pinned to the bulletin board were ads for apartments, a Chevy Camaro, and a VCR. The VCR ad had lots of little paper tabs at the bottom that said: VCR $50—355-7898. I ripped one off, went back outside, and sat on the step. I didn't want to buy a VCR, but maybe if the person who was selling it noticed a tab was missing, he would be happy.

Hope came out a few minutes later.

"I'm going to the record place. Wanna come?"

"Sure." I stood up and stuck the paper in my pocket.

"We've gotta lock up."

I leaned in to grab an ice cube before locking my door.

Hope opened the hatchback again and reached for yet another brown paper bag; this one was small and very rumpled. The moment had the look of something sneaky.

I followed her across the street to an old brick building, through a heavy glass door that said THE RECORD COLLECTOR, and up a flight of stairs. The muffled sound of music came through a set of double doors that was plastered with small posters advertising bands like the Flamingo Lips and Bad Stink. Next to the doors was a rack with copies of a little newspaper called *Slow Fish*. Hope grabbed one, but I didn't. I was afraid it might mean something, or I would be yelled at because I hadn't paid for it.

Hope jerked open the door, and loud music and cold air sprayed over us like the blast from the horn on the speeding truck.

At the counter, a guy was making notes on an envelope and didn't seem to care whether or not he had customers. Hope walked over to him and opened the bag, still looking like a thief I thought. I wasn't sure I wanted to know what was going on, so I wandered over to a rack under a USED BLUES TAPES sign. It seemed early in the trip to buy anything really important. After all, we were still in Iowa.

I flipped through the plastic cases, picked up *On the Road Again* by Willie Nelson, and put it down. I checked my compass and saw that I was facing east, so I turned toward the OLD NEW-AGE CDS, where I could face west.

I looked over at Hope, and she and the guy at the counter were smiling at each other and pointing at one of the CDs, maybe flirting while they haggled over a price. Gross. I wanted to get out. A kid with a ripped blue T-shirt was looking through the rack of music next to me. He saw me glance at him, and he winked. Double gross. I headed for the counter. Hope took some bills the guy handed her, caught my eye, and tipped her head toward the door. Saved.

4

Hope went back into the Laundromat, and I sat down in the car with the door open. I'd forgotten how hot it was outside. The humidity made me feel like I was dripping from everywhere. It was like the Earth was sweating. Besides being hot, I was frustrated. Traveling without doing any actual moving bugs me.

I checked the odometer. It should have been 126,555 plus about 60 miles. But it wasn't. Not a thing had changed. I'd have to keep track of everything with my map.

After a while Hope came out of the Laundromat again. "The stuff's in the dryer. It shouldn't be long."

"Your odometer is broken. No mileage change since we left Davenport."

"Are you sure?"

"Didn't it end in five five five? It still does."

She sighed. "I wonder when that happened."

"Why would that church have no windows, Hope?" I asked, pointing at the yellow structure.

"It wasn't always a church. I remember when it was a place where you could give blood and get money for it."

"Really?"

Hope and I were standing there, staring at the blood building, when a squawking blue jay flew over us so close that Hope flinched.

"What?!" She put her hand to her head and pulled it away fast. "NO!" she yelled. "Bird poop!"

I tried not to laugh, but I couldn't help it.

"Shut up! What'll I do?!" she shrieked, horror shrinking her face into a prune.

"Come on, isn't there water in here?"

"A washing machine?" She sounded like she was going to cry.

"Isn't there a bathroom?"

I led her to the back of the Laundromat where—better than the bathroom—there was a deep plastic laundry tub with a long faucet. I pointed. "Duck."

"Why didn't you tell me that a few minutes ago?" She forced a chuckle.

I helped her soak her hair and went back to the car.

When she came out I was making up a song about the bluebird of happiness, of haplessness, of hopelessness, of mopiness. She smiled, and then we both actually laughed.

Soon we were waiting at a red light on our way back to 80 when Hope cried out, "Oh no," and dropped behind the steering wheel.

"What's wrong?" I watched a tall guy in khaki shorts and a gray T-shirt walk by the car. To me, he was just another stranger, so I looked at him hard, trying to see what had upset Hope.

She hissed, "Never mind!"

"What's the big deal?"

"Tell me when he's gone."

I circled my fingers around my eyes like binoculars and spoke in the voice of a spy. "Continuing to stride across pavement, approaching curb, raising right foot, he's up! Marching along pavement like he owns the block, disappearing behind large, bark-covered tree—"

"That's enough." Hope sat up.

"Jeez, Hope. He looked kind of cute to me."

"Once upon a time he looked pretty cute to me, too."

"Yeah?"

"Was he why you left Iowa City?"

"Sort of."

"Is that why you move? First, it was Davenport to Iowa City, then Atlanta, Georgia, of all places, Chicago, and now, suddenly, it's Reno."

"Don't be so smug about it. Moving's great," she said. "You've been in Davenport, Iowa, your whole life, and you're only thirteen."

"Summers in Reno, don't forget," I said in a stern voice. I didn't care if I was younger. I had a life, too.

"Well, to get it right, you might remember that I began life in Madison, Wisconsin, years before Davenport."

I shut my mouth. Sometimes I *did* forget that Hope had a history before I was born.

I pulled a fresh piece of ice from the half-melted cubes to rub on my neck. In front of us was a van with the license plate, B8NFSH—*Bait and fish.* Very cute. What would I want to say on a license plate? I took out my notebook and wrote down the alphabet and numbers and began playing with seven spaces. Something about being organized. 2GETHER. Except that *together* sounded like something a couple would put on their car.

Maybe something about travel, like UZEMAPS. I tried to think of how I could get the idea *I'd rather be flying* into seven slots. FLYDON'TDRIVE didn't shrink very well. FLY2RENO was even too long. DON'TDRIVEWITHHOPE would take several license plates.

"Look," Hope said. She pointed at the back window of the car in front of us. I saw three circles the size of little pancakes. Each one appeared to be made from black threads, like spiderwebs, with a solid black spider in the middle.

"They're fake bullet holes. Must be some plastic thing you can stick on windows."

I looked harder and saw what she saw—holes surrounded by shattered glass. "That's sick. Why would somebody want to pretend they've got bullet holes in their car? I never see stuff like this in Davenport."

"That's traveling for you," said Hope. "They say it's supposed to broaden you."

"Broaden or flatten?"

We pulled out to pass the car. When we were even, I saw that the driver was sitting stiff and wearing a camouflage outfit—even his cap.

"Pass him."

She did, and I quietly said, "Thank you."

We rode for a long time without saying much. On the other side of the freeway, the cars and trucks heading east were suddenly overcome by dozens of motorcyclists. Their black helmets and cycles made them seem like large, noisy insects rushing down the road. Beyond the sounds of traffic on the road, the fields looked peaceful—new cornstalks marking places in the soil, road signposts set deep in the ground, farms here and there. One tall roadside tree was shaped like a poodle. It must have been an accident, like clouds, but it almost looked like a special trim job. Every once in a while, I'd see a clump of hay or a garbage bag caught on some weeds, and I'd yell, "Look!" I always thought it was something dead until we were right next to it. Hope said I was nuts. Once, though, it was a real tennis shoe. Only one.

After a while, I pulled out the Iowa map to see how far we'd gone. Pitiful progress, but I said nothing. Instead I tried to create whatever order I could by carefully tucking the pleats of the map back into its accordion folds, doubling it over, and sliding it back into place in my backpack. I pulled the zipper all the way and laid the backpack to the right of my feet—away from the melting ice. My space. It was the only thing I could control.

I inhaled as deeply as I could and counted to ten. I wondered how many times I could count to ten between Davenport and Reno.

"Let's hit a truck stop," Hope said finally. "Time for a bathroom break for me. I don't know about you." We pulled into the lot, and Hope jumped out of the car and raced to the other end of the lot and back. "You ought to get some exercise. It feels good."

I said nothing and followed her inside. A skinny guy with beady eyes was peering into a glass case with hunting knives. He looked up as Hope and I walked by and gave us a creepy smile. We hurried into the bathroom and made ugly faces at each other. When we came out, he was gone, and while Hope bought a snack, I raced outside and slipped behind the van parked next to us, did ten jumping jacks really fast, and then leaned on the car, waiting for her, like I hadn't moved a muscle.

Outside, we opened cans of tuna and some pop. Lunch.

As we pulled back onto the freeway, Hope turned on the radio, which went from static to fuzz. "Shoot, it was working this morning." She clicked it off with a sharp twist.

Sort of working, I thought, but I didn't say anything.

"Must have some Cheetos," Hope said in a deep, silly voice, and ripped open the bag that she'd bought at the truck stop. She ate or rather *stuffed* a bunch of the lumpy curls into her mouth and then waved her orange fingers in the air.

"Want a napkin?" I said.

She looked at me like she'd never heard such a stupid question and started sucking the coating off each finger. When she swiped them across her purple shorts, they left fuzzy stripes of orange crumbs.

"Want some?" she asked.

"No," I snapped.

———

Eventually, Hope was actually driving around Des Moines, with its snaky exits leading off one side of the freeway, then the other. Yellow signs saying, THIS LANE, EXIT ONLY made me nervous about staying on 80, but Hope didn't drive off once—accidentally or on purpose. Still, the day felt like one of the longest ones I'd ever lived. Mom's reassuring words—*You'll be halfway across Nebraska before nightfall*—seemed to have been spoken days ago, not just hours. We still had a few hours before we'd be out of Iowa.

I reached for the map to figure things out again and updated the numbers.

Distance from Davenport—255 miles
Distance to Reno—1,508 miles

Then I began a list of every county we passed through. Scott, Cedar, Johnson, Iowa, Poweshiek, Jasper, Polk, and into Dallas. Hope's eyes were riveted to the road, and I kept my mouth shut as the miles behind us grew. After a while I added Madison and Adair counties to my list. We were getting closer to the Iowa-Nebraska border, but we'd never get through Iowa *and* halfway across the next state before we slept. I was sure of it.

The apple core was dark and shriveled. Like my heart, I thought. Ick. That idea was too full of self-pity, even for me, and I laughed at myself. The late afternoon sun was booming into the car, and the simple act of breathing made me feel like I was at the edge of a volcano sucking in scorched air.

Hope flipped on the fan for the broken air conditioner again. The air coming out of the vents was the same air that was coming in the windows. "Let's get out of this heat for a while," she suggested. "Ever been to Atlantic?"

5

A green and white highway sign said that ATLANTIC was the next exit. Hope pulled off and headed south. The town was six miles in, according to a small sign.

Riding on a two-lane road made me nervous. I looked at my compass, knowing what I'd see. South. I wanted her to be driving *with* the speeding traffic going *west.* Every other direction was wrong. I untangled another hair from my brush and let it slip out the window. *Find me, magic DNA camera. If I get lost, find me.*

We drove down Main Street where people strolled in and out of restaurants, a hardware store, the library, and other shops. Hope looked left and right at every corner and then saw something down one of the streets that tugged at her attention, and she turned left.

"So what's this job Dad has for you?" I asked. I'd thought about asking earlier, but each time I remembered, one of us was too grumpy or something else was going on.

"For a nightclub in a casino." She was distracted, driving down the strange street slowly. "Assistant costume designer."

"A casino! Those places are gross. Besides, I thought

you wanted to design clothes for Gen Y-ers or whatever you call yourselves."

"I need a *job*, Carin," she snapped. "The money's decent, and it'll expand me."

"A casino?"

"Listen, Carin, it's an incredible job. The styles, the fabrics, and . . . never mind. Forget it."

In front of us was a large park. A flapping banner stretched above the street read: WELCOME CLASSES 1990—2000!!

"Well, look at that," Hope said. "We've stumbled onto a high school reunion. A perfect party."

"What?" I said, feeling muddled.

"Lots of food, lots of people who don't know each other."

I wondered what she had in mind; it didn't feel good, but the smell of grilled meat filled the air, and I felt a sudden craving. Hope turned a corner, and a sea of cars fanned out before us on what seemed like an endless lawn. Hope found a space and slipped in. "Let's go."

I followed, but I was confused. "Where are we going?"

"Jesse Cutler—a guy I knew in Chicago."

Jesse Cutler. Hmmm. I found myself happy to be out of the car, walking along on thick grass in slightly cooler air.

A long grill was surrounded by men and women in striped aprons and poofy, mushroom-shaped hats flipping burgers and chicken. The chefs' graceful and clever handling of tongs reminded me of dealers in casinos, sliding chips around the craps table with their long wands.

37

We went a little farther, and Hope approached some people with plastic plates piled with food. "Have you seen Jesse Cutler?" she asked.

The people all shook their heads slowly, and a few said, "Jesse Cutler?" One of them, a big guy with dark hair and a plaid shirt, added, "Are you sure it's this class? This is '95."

"See," one of them said, using his fork to point to a tree, "our sign fell down."

Hope cocked her head sideways. "Maybe I'm wrong. Actually, I'm not sure which—"

"And you're—?"

"Hope Tate."

Tate! Our last name was Mullins. What was she up to? My face was growing red, and it wasn't from the heat.

Hope pressed on. "You're—"

"Todd Bronberg," he said slowly, pointing at his name tag.

"Sure," Hope continued. "We were in choir together. I was only here for a semester. Then we moved to Daven-port."

Todd shrugged. "Well, grab some food while you're looking for what's-his-name."

"Thanks. Jesse Cutler."

Hope steered us to the table and we each picked up a plate. It seemed weird to be doing this, but my mouth was watering.

"Hope—" I said.

She leaned close to my face. "There *is* a Jesse Cutler who

38

may or may not be here. In the meanwhile, I don't particularly want to give away my life story. Okay?"

I nodded. *Sure, why not. Just one more weird thing in a weird day.*

Making our way down both sides of the table, we helped ourselves to pasta and potato salads, pickles and olives, slices of cheese, grapes and strawberries, and, finally, grilled burgers in a large serving dish with little feet. I took a patty, a large bun, a tomato slice, and mustard.

We sat down under a tree, and I began eating like a wild child, not caring a bit how I looked. Hope got drinks—root beer for me and ginger ale for her.

I finally slowed down and looked around. "Hope, it looks like we're the only people here without name tags. See?" I watched her to make sure she was looking, too. "And you have to admit our dress is a bit more casual than most of the Atlantic alums."

"Yes," she said as she stuffed her own mouth.

"We're stealing food, aren't we, Hope?" I said, suddenly overcome with guilt, now that I wasn't so hungry.

Hope pursed her lips. "Here's the story. We didn't receive an engraved invitation. On the other hand, we're giving them an opportunity to share the wealth. You saw all the food there. No way are there enough hungry people in Atlantic to devour it all. It'll be chucked."

I knew she was right, but that didn't make our self-help feeding program right. "It's still stealing."

"You always have the choice of paying for it some way. Do something."

The guy named Todd dropped down by us with a fresh soda for Hope. "Weren't you big in art? I'd bet anything on it.

Some people with aprons carried trays of ice cream cups to the table. A woman holding one of the trays was looking helplessly at the table as if her stare alone might clear enough space for the ice cream. I jumped up to help, slid some salads close to each other, and piled a nearly empty fruit plate on top of a nearly empty veggie plate. She smiled at me and set the tray down. I stacked the little cups two and three high and went out to work the crowd, doling out the treats and gathering the garbage.

When I finished dumping the last of the plates into a heaping trash can, I felt that I'd paid for my supper, and I helped myself to a paper cup of what I knew would be ice cream soup. Since it was chocolate, it tasted like a warmish milk shake. Perfect enough.

When I returned to the tree, Hope and Todd were yukking it up.

"Carin," Hope said, full of cheer. "Hey, Todd has a brother in Wyoming he says we've got to visit."

More strangers? No thanks. "Are we going to leave soon?"

"Sure. Pretty soon."

"I'm going for a walk." I had to get away from them.

"Don't get lost."

It's Atlantic, Iowa, if you haven't noticed. How far could I go?

As I turned away, Hope began another story about the time she and her friends moved to Atlanta, and they were hit by a freak snowstorm on the way. *That* story was actually true.

Wandering around in a strange place made me feel disconnected from everything I knew. If Hope appeared right now and I pretended not to know her, would it mean I could be sisterless? If she'd actually become Hope Tate, I *would* be sisterless. Was having a sister a condition? It felt like a disease sometimes. Was there a cure?

I walked to the car to get my bearings, lifted the compass, and held it as steady as I could. The needle shivered as it pointed north. I walked west.

I wove through the lines of cars and wondered if I should call Mom and have her come and get me. She'd be ticked that we were still in Iowa. Dad, too. Maybe I should call him. Before long, I found myself in a distant part of the park with no one around.

Behind some trees, I came to a fountain the size of a big dining-room table. It looked so inviting that I slipped out of my sandals and stepped in. The cool water was a wonderful shock. I kicked and splashed and perched on the edge so I could flip more water on my legs. It was peaceful here even though it was a little scary to think that no one knew where I was. It reminded me of another park Hope had taken me to years earlier.

It was July Fourth. Mom and Dad had gone with friends on a boat ride on the Mississippi, and Hope and her buddies went to City Park to grill burgers and hot dogs before the fireworks.

She took me along, but at the park, she was so busy flipping burgers and goofing off with her friends that I could have strolled right into the pond and drowned. I headed alone to the bathroom, which meant going up a big hill, away from the crowds, and across the parking lot, which felt spooky with all the empty cars. I was gone for a long time. When I got back, I walked over to her, and she just said "hi" as if nothing'd happened, like I hadn't even been gone.

Eventually she asked me if I wanted a hamburger—it was a miracle that any were left. I took one and put lots of mustard on it and on my plate, too. I loved mustard, not only on food but on forks or spoons or even fingers. I ate a bite of hamburger and then slurped three or four spoonfuls of mustard. She didn't notice, of course. I could have been splatted flat on the road and she wouldn't have noticed.

Later, she had to notice me, but not because she wanted to. I was standing by the ladder at the kids' slide when I threw up. Kids started screaming, because what landed on the ground was bright yellow from all the mustard. They were screaming that I was an alien. I started crying. Hope took me home, and she was mad. No more grilling, no fireworks, no hanging out with her old and new friends.

She told me to go to bed in such a loud voice that I didn't dare get up, even though I felt much better. I heard her downstairs for a while, banging around the kitchen, playing tapes, and then, after it grew dark, I heard the door close and a car engine start.

I slipped out of bed and went into the hall. The bathroom light was on, and long shadows reached across the floor and up the walls. I crept downstairs. "Hope?" I called quietly. I couldn't believe she'd actually gone.

There was no answer. "Hope!" This time I said it louder, and the echo of my own voice seemed to tumble over the furniture and circle back to my lonely self. I went to the kitchen and looked out the door. The car was gone. Hope was gone. I was alone. And no one would come home for a long time.

I was afraid, but I wanted to be brave and to take care of myself. I went to the living room and sat down on the couch. I didn't turn lights on because I didn't want anyone to look in and see me alone. Sitting in the dark made me tired, I guess, and I fell asleep. But fireworks began to go off. At first, I thought bombs were exploding. I jumped up, screamed, and hid behind a chair. I didn't want to cry, but I couldn't help it.

Hope had gotten in trouble, of course. But as the years passed, I wasn't sure if I'd been more scared being home alone or if I'd felt worse at the picnic where she was laughing and talking to total strangers but didn't seem to know or care where I was.

I stopped daydreaming and lifted one foot out of the water. My skin had started pruning. Time to find Hope. The sun was tipping lower in the sky; maybe we could go.

I pulled on my sandals and headed back to the parking area. Lots of cars had left, leaving holes here and there, like a checkerboard when the game's half over. I looked for a huge red pickup truck because the Escort had been parked next to it. But I couldn't see the truck. I started feeling confused about where we'd parked. I walked up one aisle and down another, crossing back and forth, back and forth.

It was dawning on me that I had lost both the truck and the Ford. "Hope!" I shouted stupidly, even though she and the car were gone. Where?!

My heart raced as I ran and stumbled toward the road that led back to Main Street. How could Hope do this? Did she go off with somebody?

Tears were streaming down my cheeks. I couldn't help it. I was mad and scared all at once. I didn't want to be stuck in Atlantic. I wanted to be in that stupid, old rusty Escort heading west. I wanted to go to Reno!

A horn suddenly honked.

"Carin! Carin!"

My stomach lurched, and I turned. Hope had pulled up across the street and was stepping out of the car. I started toward her and she ran to me. "Where *were* you?! Where did you go!?"

"Oh dear. Carin, I'm so sorry. I just went for gas." She reached up to wipe my tears away. "What awful timing."

"You can say that again." I was so glad to see her that my anger melted. "I thought you'd left me."

Hope put her arm around me. "I'd never do that. I am so sorry. Come on."

We walked back to the car.

"We'd better make a pact, okay? From now on"—she

seemed to be hunting for the right words—"the car will stay put until we're both in it. Let's get back to the freeway."

I didn't need any urging. I hopped in my side of the car, then took the wishbone from home out of my backpack and tucked it into my pocket—something I should have done long ago.

As Hope started the engine, she looked at me. "Sorry, Carin."

I shrugged.

She pulled the car into traffic and headed north to the interstate. The sun was setting, and the harsh heat with it. We drove along quietly in the dusky light, putting mile after mile behind us.

After what felt like a long while, Hope said, "Hey, hungry?"

"Yes. It feels like hours since the picnic food."

"It *has* been hours."

She eased into a small town and drove slowly along Main Street looking for a restaurant. When she turned off the car, we headed into the Flying A Eatery where nearly all the booths were filled with merry customers in baseball uniforms, and the smell of fried chicken curled through the summer air.

6

When we stepped out of the Flying A Eatery, our stomachs filled once again, it was dark. We each clutched a small plastic bubble from a gumball machine. Hope's was full of green fuzz, and it looked like mine had a little clothesline with tiny clothespins. I couldn't wait to put it up.

"Where are we sleeping?" I asked.

"I don't know. Let's drive for a while."

We took off and soon turned west again toward Council Bluffs, the last city on the western edge of Iowa. As we drove along, the red rear lights on the cars and trucks in front of us glowed like the night eyes of animals. It was as if we were traveling together in a pack, racing backwards to the Missouri River, the end of Iowa and the beginning of Nebraska.

"Man, am I ever tired," Hope said after a while.

I said nothing. I wished we were closer to Reno, but at least we were in the car together heading in the right direction.

Hope pulled off the freeway when we reached the outskirts of Council Bluffs and drove along the frontage road.

The businesses were all closed—car repair, tire places, warehouses for who-knew-what. "Hey, this is handy." She whipped into a used-car lot and parked at the end of a row of cars.

"What are you doing?"

"Let me take a little nap, okay? Just ten or fifteen minutes. Then we'll get going again."

"It's almost ten."

"Just a teensy nap and we'll find a motel. I'm beat, Carin. I left Chicago at six-thirty this morning."

I knew Hope was tired, but this wacky idea seemed so typical of her—a nap in the car when we should be in a motel.

"Well, I'm not going to sleep, so let's swap seats and you can stretch out."

"Okay."

I got out and walked around the car, and she clambered over the middle. When I slid into her seat, she was already leaning against the passenger door and breathing heavily. I couldn't believe it. Day one of *the sister adventure* and we were still in Iowa.

I glanced at Hope—my *older* sister, who was supposed to be the responsible one here. She was snoring peacefully, *peacefully*. Hopeless was what she was. Not Hope. I leaned back and sighed, then twisted around to lock the door. Out of the corner of my eye, I noticed again the sign taped on the back passenger window, WESTWARD HO! Not likely. WESTWARD HOPELESS made more sense.

I yanked the sign off, pulled pens out of my backpack, and quickly added a PELESS to HO. I studied it, crossed out WARD, and wrote WITH above it. There. WEST WITH HOPELESS. Much more accurate. I taped the sign back in place.

The night-lights of the sales lot sparkled on cars' clean windows and chrome strips. Even though I was sure nothing about this car sparkled, it seemed like we'd become part of a department store display. I watched the traffic on the frontage road. Since there was a stoplight nearby, cars slowed and stopped every time the light turned red. A few people glanced our way, but their looks were brief and mostly empty.

Even though I didn't think I'd fall asleep, I was suddenly jolted awake by a loud crack on the window. I nearly jumped through the roof, and so did Hope. The car was filled with the beam from a strong flashlight. Hope grabbed my arm and my stomach took a dive.

Whoever was holding the flashlight tapped it again on the window, and I rolled it down an inch. The policeman turned the light on himself; I was relieved to see the uniform.

"What are you girls doing out here?"

"Heading for Nebraska, Officer," Hope said, Miss Alertness. My eyes went wide. *Nebraska?* Why Nebraska, and how could she sound so awake?

"Can I see your license?" He was looking at me. My stomach churned.

Hope again rose to the occasion. "Sir, I'm the driver

here. My sister volunteered to take the tight space so I could catch a few winks." Hope found her purse and produced her license. *A few winks.*

He glanced at it and passed it back. "The owner of this business doesn't take kindly to motorists sleeping on the premises."

Hope nodded vigorously. "I understand, Officer. We'll head on down the road."

He pointed in the obvious direction. "There're motels down a few miles. Maybe they'd give you a bargain rate, since it's so late." He smiled at me.

"That'd be nice. We'll check it out," Hope said, with one foot out the passenger door.

"Thank you," I said.

He walked back to his car and started his engine. I got out.

She leaned toward the car clock. "Three-thirty. Oh, this was a bad idea." She slowly came around to her side, rubbing her neck and wobbling a bit.

I wanted to agree with her in a big way, but it was so dark and so late. We slipped into our usual seats. Hope shoved the car into gear and sprayed gravel as she spun us back onto the frontage road that would lead to motels and big, soft beds. I could hardly wait.

"There's no such thing as a bargain at a motel for half a night," Hope muttered to herself as she drove on. In the glow of the dashboard lights, I could see she was working her eyebrows up and down and stretching her forehead muscles. Trying to wake up, I thought. She headed toward Council Bluffs and turned right at a stoplight a few miles down the road. "Watch for motels."

We passed an all-night pancake house, some gas stations, and a few fast-food places, but nothing that looked like a motel.

"Man, he didn't give very good directions." Hope turned down a side street, and then into an alley, stopping finally behind a gas station. There were lots of cars parked this way and that, and it was dark except for streetlights.

"What *are* you doing, Hope?"

"I'm sorry, Carin. I'm beat. We're going to have a wreck if I have to drive around looking for a motel. It's only a few more hours. Please."

"So we're sleeping here? In the car?"

"'Fraid so. Worse things have happened."

"Not to me."

"You're a lucky dog then. Sleep," she commanded and gave me a big goofy smile. That was all. There was no room for argument. This car—the Hotel Escort—was going to be *it* for the whole night. I reached under the seat for the Whitman's Sampler, not because I was hungry but for something to do. I couldn't even read the chart to see what I was eating; I just shoved several pieces of candy in my mouth and ate them as loudly as I could, though it didn't seem to keep Hope from falling into another deep sleep.

Hope was already leaning toward her door, her legs pulled up, her mouth half-open. I rolled down my window a crack for ventilation, because what if we ran out of oxygen while we slept. Bad end.

The night air was cooler. The buzz of crickets and hum bugs was a gentle drone, the same sounds I listened to when I was falling asleep in my own bed. My own bed. I ignored the sting of tears I suddenly felt on my eyes and concentrated on sleep.

7

We awoke to the *ding-a-ling* of the gas station bell and the sun pouring through the windshield. Ugh. I sat up and wiped the slobber off my chin. I hate when that happens.

"Breakfast?" Hope said.

"What about a shower?" I lifted an arm; it stuck to my shirt, which was sticking to my chest.

"Yeah." She sniffed the air. "Yeah, I'd say, but we can't do that until a public pool opens. It could be noon."

"Don't sniff *my* air. *Your* breath could crumple buildings."

"We're quite the pair, aren't we?"

"And we're still in Iowa." I felt a wave of self-pity—a terrible way to start the day.

"Nebraska," Hope said without sarcasm, which was nice of her. "I promise you we'll get across Nebraska before the sun sets."

I wondered if, like her other promises, this one would be hopeless, too.

Before we left the station, we opened our plastic bubbles. I wound the ends of the little clothesline around the braces that held the sun visors to the car. The tiny plastic clothespins bobbed on the string, waiting for souvenirs. Hope's prize was a long, fuzzy green strip with two little glass beads glued to one end.

"It must be a snake," I said.

"Are there good-luck snakes, Carin?"

"I'm sure there are. Somewhere."

She wound it around her visor. "Then let's declare ourselves to be in that Somewhere."

I grabbed the top of my hand and pinched myself. We were actually out of Iowa and driving through Omaha. The freeway widened into several lanes with nearly constant on-ramps and off-ramps. I hated how squashed I felt when we were in the center lane and giant trucks pulled up on both sides. Billboards advertising the rain forest and desert at the zoo kept popping up at every turn. Hope started babbling about going to the zoo, which I would have loved, but I knew that if we got off the road, it would be hours before we got back on—hours and hours.

"Are you *sure* you don't want to go to the zoo? Rain forest? Desert? Meercats?" Hope asked, for the third time. "You know you'd love it."

"I *know* I would, but we'd lose too much time."

She'd promised we'd get across Nebraska before nightfall, and I didn't want to be the one to blame if it didn't happen. I kept my eye out for every sign that said 80 west, and I yelled out which lane she should be in. There were lots of those signs.

"PLEASE stop telling me which lane to get in."

I said something three more times and then stopped. But I felt my persistence had paid off as we left Omaha behind us.

I took out my atlas again and figured out where we were.

Distance from Davenport—301 miles
Distance to Reno—1,462 miles

After I wrote down the numbers, I put things away. "Too bad we can't polish our nails. That would give us something to do."

"While driving?" Hope said with her eyebrows raised.

"Maybe."

"You wild woman, you. Hey, are there any sparkling waters left?" Hope asked.

I twisted in my seat to get to the cooler and found the last two cans bobbing around. I couldn't help but think of the marshmallows bobbing in my cocoa just a day and a half ago. The thought made me feel a little homesick, so I pushed it away as I shook off the water and handed her a can. "These are the last two. We could use another bag of ice in there, too."

Hope held the can to her cheek. "And gas."

At the next exit, we pulled off for our first stop of the day. As Hope pushed the gas nozzle into the tank hole, I heard her burst out laughing. She'd seen the sign. "Some art gremlin at work here? *West with Hopeless,* eh?" she called.

"Just keeping myself busy in those late hours."

When she got back in the car, she gave me a friendly cuff on the shoulder. "You goofball."

In a few minutes we were back on the road, and it began to feel like we were in the rhythm of long-distance driving. We didn't talk much. The list of counties grew. Douglas, Sarpy, Cass, Lancaster. Hope had easily navigated around Lincoln and I'd kept my mouth shut. We were leaving behind anything that resembled a city and plunging into what seemed like a vast space dotted with tiny towns, banded by the long, slow curve of Interstate 80 as it crossed Nebraska. Along both sides of the highway were wide ditches, some filled with shining water, and beyond them were thick clumps of trees. It made me feel as if we were being escorted down a long, wide hallway toward our destination.

I reached for the Whitman's Sampler box again and was surprised at how light it was. Only a few pieces left. I offered some to Hope and we ate our way through the rest of the chocolates. I took the last brown paper cup, flattened the fluted sides as much as I could, and clipped it to the clothesline.

"That's a good souvenir, even if you brought it from home," said Hope.

And now I had a cool yellow box to do something wonderful with. I shoved it under my seat, where I could easily reach it as soon as I came up with the wonderful idea.

Once in a while, along the side of the road, I'd see what looked like a platform for a New Jersey train stop. Such a structure seemed weird in the middle of Nebraska. I knew about the elevated platforms in New Jersey because Dad had once taken me to visit his cousin in the East.

The Nebraska versions had metal railings on both sides of a long path that led to the platforms, and all of it was surrounded by a fence. I ignored the first one, but we passed more and more, and finally one was being used. There wasn't a train in sight. Instead, several trucks were lined up near the platform, and one was backed up to it. Cattle walked up the ramp, across the platform, into the trailer and, no doubt, on to the slaughterhouse. After seeing them loaded like that, I felt a little sick each time we passed another platform—even though they were empty, and I wondered if maybe I should become a vegetarian after all.

"Still interested in a shower?" Hope asked after a while.

"Yes, definitely."

She studied the road as if we were driving through a fog. "Well, I have an idea," she said, and veered into the exit lane for some tiny town. Almost immediately she whipped the car into a three-bay car wash. Shoot. I didn't feel like cleaning this old rust bucket. I started rolling up my window. "Skip that," she said. "Take off your sandals and get out."

"What?"

"It's *shower* time. Come on." She popped quarters into the coin slot and lifted the hose from its hooks. "Wanna go first?"

"A car wash?" I said, suddenly realizing her plan.

"Hey, it's water and soap. Dirty cars or stinky kids. What's the difference?"

I laughed.

"Get over there, the far side. You know about the pressure in these things."

I obeyed.

"Here goes. Close your eyes and keep twirling."

The water stung a little but it felt great. After a minute of the soap cycle, Hope gave me the hose to squirt her and she ran to where I'd been standing. I resisted the temptation to push the power button, since she hadn't done it to me. It might have ripped a hole right through her.

We switched to "rinse" and the water switched to freezing cold. Aah. Some people had driven into the lot during the rinse cycle, and they were laughing their heads off. I thought they were probably laughing at us, not with us, but I didn't care. The water felt that good.

"Just a little road sweat," Hope said to the strangers as she put the nozzle back into the wall brackets. Of course she had to talk to them.

We pulled dry clothes out of our bags, changed in the restroom, spread out the wet things over the cooler, and popped into the car.

"Thanks, Hope."

"Yeah? Two clean girls for only a buck and a quarter."

She zipped the car back onto the freeway. "And in under ten minutes."

We drove on, refreshed and quiet for a while until Hope suddenly pointed at some dark lump in a field.

"Look over there," she said. "Is that a small steer or a big black pib?"

"Pib?" I asked.

"Pig."

"You said pib."

"No, I said pig. Pig is what I meant."

"You might *mean* pig, but you said pib," I said.

"All right, all right, I said pib. My lips are stupid."

"The three little pibs. The little pibby who went to market."

"Okay, okay. But what was it? A steer or a piG?"

I shrugged. "Didn't see it."

She took a swing at me, but she was laughing so hard, she whacked her elbow instead. "My crazy bone! Hold the wheel! Hold the wheel!"

"You're not fit to drive," I teased.

"And you're not fit to be a passenger!" She took the wheel back. "Okay. Back to the business at hand. Driving from Davenport to Reno. On we go."

8

We were deep into a road rhythm and a few hours slipped by. I finished weaving the embroidery-thread bracelet for Jenna and looked into the hot, cloudless sky.

For something to do, I studied the map again and filled in my county list with new names: Seward, York, Hamilton, Hall, and Buffalo. After a while nature called, and Hope wasn't answering. I was nice twice, and then I lost patience. "Hope! How many times do I have to say it? I need to pee!" Suddenly I felt like I'd been complaining for a very long time, because that's what it feels like when you need a bathroom. Hope had driven right past two exits.

"Okay, okay. I thought you were just planning ahead or bored or something. So should I stop the car here? In the middle of nowhere?"

I couldn't wait any longer. "Yes, yes! Here. Now!"

"All right, all right." The car began to slow.

"Not in front of a pond!"

She scowled and made some kind of spitting sound. It was now or never. The car finally stopped. Not far off was a stand of trees, and I pushed open the door and was jumping through the weedy ditch when I heard Hope yell, "Kleenex?"

"Drat," I muttered and raced back to my backpack. "I hate you." Only a sister would think you were "bored" when you said you had to pee.

She laughed. "Just trying to help."

I ran to the trees and squatted in the brush. The relief was huge. It was a miracle I hadn't burst open.

Looking back through the branches, I could see Hope leaning against the car like she was on a movie set. The heat made the air above the pavement quiver and her ankles seemed to shimmy, the same way they would have looked in a swimming pool.

In the other direction was a field of some short young plant, maybe soybeans. Beyond the field was a huge building that, by the smell, I figured was full of pigs eating their days away. Now *that's* boring—doing nothing but getting ready to walk that last stretch into the trucks, headed for pork chop land. If they knew their destiny, they'd stampede to the ocean. I wondered if pigs could swim.

As I looked back at Hope, a low black car with a spoiler pulled up. Uh-oh. Where was this movie going? I yanked up my shorts, grabbed the Kleenex pack, and headed to the highway, each step taking me closer to the drama. Mom always said not to buy a used car like the one I was staring at because they're usually owned by guys who show off when they're driving—laying rubber and stuff like that. She thinks they're more *used* than most used cars. I climbed through the weeds across the gully.

"And here's my sister, Carin," Hope said, laughing in a flirty way and ignoring the fact that maybe I didn't want to be introduced to a couple of geeky strangers along the highway, college boys or whatever they were with their baseball caps on backwards.

Cars zipped by and hot exhaust filled my nose.

"So you don't need any help?" the taller guy said.

"Not unless you could zap us to Reno," Hope said.

I thought that was a dumb thing to say, but Hope always found *something* to say.

We got back in the car and the boys got in their car, and that was that.

Hope started the engine. "They stopped to see if we were in trouble. That was nice, wasn't it."

"Yeah, I guess so." I just couldn't feel as comfortable with strangers as Hope did.

She pulled back onto the pavement. "So how much money did Cathy give you for emergencies this time?" she asked after a while.

"None of your beeswax." I was irritated at having to pee in the weeds, and my mood came right out of my mouth.

"Oh, that's mature," she grumbled. "How little are you?"

Little, she calls me. *I'm* taller. I regretted saying "beeswax." It did make me sound like a snotty little kid.

We drove on like that. The mood had swung again. It didn't matter much if we were talking or not. These little spikes of irritation flew around the car like porcupine quills. I knew porcupines couldn't fire them off, but a lot of people think they can, and if they could, this was what it would feel like. Maybe the heat was getting to us. Sometimes you could see why hot weather by itself seemed to make people want to fight.

I took some gum out of my bag, gave some to Hope as a peace token, and rolled up a stick before popping it in my mouth. I fiddled with the metallic wrapper, for something to do, folding it and unfolding it. When I pressed it flat again, it looked like a map of a river with lots of tributaries.

Suddenly I got an idea for Grams's Whitman Sampler box—a relief map like we made in the fifth grade. Instead of a salt-and-flour mix, I could use gum. I was so happy about my new idea that I stopped thinking about fighting with Hope.

Since my favorite thing about Whitman Samplers was the "map" inside the top of the box, where circles and squares and rectangles were arranged like the candies, it seemed like fun to make a different kind of map on the bottom. Thinking about maps made me think of the old map from my bedroom wall—especially the section with no borders that was labeled "Neutral Ground." Where were Hope and I now? "Neutral Ground"? Or maybe we were in "Unknown—Perhaps Neutral, Perhaps Dangerous—Ground."

I found a pencil and sketched in the path from Davenport to Reno in the bottom of the box. I'd looked at the map so much, I knew the zigs and zags by heart. I stuck my gum down at one edge of the box and began chewing some more. I chewed enough to make about three inches worth of map, which ran from Davenport almost to the western edge of Nebraska while it was still soft. I snipped a piece of black thread from my embroidery floss and pressed it into the gum with a pencil. The thread was Interstate 80. I put it away to harden.

"Do you notice the smell, Hope?"

"Your gum?" She said.

"No. Every time we've stopped, I could smell it—more or less."

"What?"

"Cow farts, I think."

She burst out laughing. "Cow farts?"

"We heard about them when we were studying the ozone. I mean, this is major cattle country, even if there were pigs back there."

"So?"

"Nebraska. Steaks and burgers. So that must be what it is."

"That's gross," she said. "Maybe it's a factory or an oil refinery. Cow farts? Come on."

"A cow factory, yes. Something to think about next time you order a burger. One of every four cows we eat in this country is a McCow."

"How do you know all this?"

"I don't know. I just remember stuff."

Hope smiled.

I sat back waiting for the hours to pass. The roadside looked the same mile after mile—wild grasses and a few trees planted between the fields and the highway. The only things that changed were the other travelers on the road.

I let myself get numbed by the passing roadside and watched the little green mileage markers. The numbers were a slow countdown across the state—200, 199, 198. Once in a while, the large green signs showed more news. NORTH PLATTE 143 MILES, NORTH PLATTE 120 MILES, NORTH PLATTE 85 MILES. We were in Buffalo County, approaching Cozad, and soon it was NORTH PLATTE 45 MILES. What I didn't know, though, was what lay beyond North Platte. I could see no sign that read RENO 1,256 MILES TO GO AND GOOD LUCK! That's what I wanted. Instead the sun pounded on us—Hope in the driver's seat, me in the passenger's.

An SUV with a bunch of hula hoops tied on the back passed us. "Look, Hope."

"You never know what you'll see on the road," she said in a sluggish voice.

"Sorry I don't know how to drive," I said.

"Hm? No drama." She reached into what was left of our newest ice bag and rubbed a cube over her neck. I did the same.

"Hey, I need a break. How about you? And looks like we could use some fresh ice, too."

Hope pulled off at the next exit and parked on the shady side of a gas station. I raced to the ice-cream cooler and stood there getting cold till it hurt. Hope picked up two Fudgsicles, paid for them, along with a newspaper and ice, and came back to the cooler, where we chilled our insides with ice cream and our outsides with the freezing air.

Back in the car, the fresh ice bag felt like a tiny piece of the Arctic. Waves of coolness wrapped around my left thigh, while my right one was already warming up in the sun. It reminded me of standing by a campfire on a cold night and having the front of you fry while your backside freezes.

"Hey, we forgot a souvenir," she said.

We looked at each other. It was clear that neither of us felt like moving. I opened my door and reached down. I came up with a little leaf. I wrote *Somewhere in Nebraska* on it. "How's this?"

"One of a kind," she said.

I used the tiny green, plastic clothespin and clipped it next to the matchbook from a station stop, the mint toothpick in its cellophane wrapper from the Flying A Eatery, and the brown paper cup from a Whitman candy. The old apple core, still attached to the mirror, was headed into deep brown and seemed more shriveled each hour.

"See what this is all about," Hope said, flipping the newspaper onto my lap.

I pulled a metal barrette out of my backpack—a gift from Dad last summer—and pulled as much hair off my neck and into it as I could. The French braid Mom had fixed yesterday was history; I jerked the rearview mirror my way for a minute and discovered I looked quite a bit like a hedgehog. Road hair. That's the way it goes.

"The *Omaha World Herald*," I read.

"Yes?" Hope said, pulling back onto the freeway.

"Look, Hope." I pointed to the right. Next to a farmhouse, a guy in a red plaid skirt was playing a bagpipe. We couldn't hear enough to trace a tune, but it sounded beautiful across the land.

"You never would have seen that if you'd flown."

I smiled and turned my attention back to the paper. "'Woman Bandies Gun.' That's the headline. Should I read on?"

Hope gave me that look.

"Right. 'Irma James, seventy-four, was arrested yesterday following a shooting spree of sorts. James, clad in a housecoat—' What's a housecoat?"

"A bathrobe, sort of. Cotton with little designs, buttons down the front." She beamed at me. "'Twentieth-century American Utilitarian Clothing'—a first-year course. I got an A."

"Okay, okay. ' . . . slammed the screen door of her home at 4337 Birch Street, according to next-door neighbor Bonnie Marshall, and ran south toward Lincoln Avenue, yelling to passersby and firing a handgun into the air. No one was wounded, but in an unexpected accident of marksmanship, one of James' bullets shot through a power line and killed the sparrow that was allegedly sitting there. According to several eyewitnesses, James shouted, "The world's going mad!" over and over.'"

"I'd say. Witness the behavior of some of Omaha's senior citizens."

"Is that enough?" I asked.

"Is there more?"

I returned to the story. "'Neighbors of James said they

66

were shocked at her behavior. "She was the kindest woman," said Merle Popper, sixty-seven. "I never knew Irma to utter an unkind word. That woman wouldn't hurt a flea."'"

"That's what all the neighbors say about serial killers— 'nicest guy on the block.'"

"Maybe it was the heat." I folded the paper, hoping to put it away. "I think heat can do strange things to people."

"Is that it?" Hope asked. "I buy a whole paper, and you read one story? I need help. I'm tired, I'm bored. And I'm sure you don't want me looking for another alumni picnic."

I started flipping through the pages again.

"Look, Hope." A water tower with a huge smiley face stood above the small town we were passing. "Do you think everyone in town was happy about that?"

Hope glanced over. "Pretty silly, but it amuses us travelers."

I couldn't argue with that.

"I don't think I should read right now. I might get carsick."

"Puking we don't need."

I pulled open the atlas. "Where are we?"

"That was Gothenburg, where the ice cream was. Doesn't reading maps make you carsick?"

I shrugged. "The next big turnoff is North Platte. 'Big' is probably the wrong word, but it's in red print on the map and the dinky towns are in black." I flipped from one page to another, trying to imagine what the maps would look like if all the cars driving on all the roads were suddenly teeny silver dots moving along. "Are we really going to get all the way across Nebraska by tonight?"

"I promised, didn't I?"

I decided not to comment on the quality of Hope's promises or my feelings about promises. I might start another fight. "We better call Mom tonight, too, to check in." Hope nodded.

How's everything? Mom would ask. And I would tell her everything was just fine. For the time being, it was. The car was gassed up, we had a fresh bag of ice, and nobody was bleeding. Things were just fine.

I calculated our location and mileage again and wrote it in my notebook:

Distance from Davenport — 585 miles
Distance to Reno — 1,178 miles

"We're over a third of the way, Hope."

Hope started humming to herself and bopping her head. She flipped the radio dial and suddenly a station came in as clear as if someone were singing in the backseat.

"Wow, there's a miracle from the travel angel," she said.

A woman's voice sang clear and broad the song about this land being your land and my land. Hope seemed hypnotized as she held her fingers on the dial. She finally said, in a rather dreamy voice, "My mom used to sing me that song. Her voice sounded a little like this woman's."

I looked at Hope and her eyes seemed a little sparkly. She lifted her fingers from the radio dial as though it were a fragile bird's egg and touched her jade necklace. She glanced at me fast with one of those smiles that people wear when their foreheads are sort of wrinkled and they're trying to prove that they're not crying.

The noise of traffic and wind faded into the background as we listened to the rest of the song. Hope flipped the dial as soon as a DJ came on. I guessed she didn't want to know whose singing had reminded her of her mom. She twisted the dial back and forth until she found a pop station without too much static and tried to cheer up fast, like she'd pushed whatever was bothering her back into a private space. But her fingers kept playing with the stones in her necklace, the one she'd gotten from her mom.

I looked at her and noticed a tear leaning out of her eyelid. She was struggling to swallow. "Carin, sometimes I miss my mom so much." Tears flowed freely down her cheeks. "It's weird, you know? I can barely remember her, just little moments really, but what I *do* remember, and the whole idea of her—" Hope sniffed a couple of times and blew out a long breath. "She's been gone more than fifteen years. Why can I still cry about her?" She tried to smile.

I felt so bad for Hope. "Well, how could you ever get used to missing somebody? Even if you got used to their being gone."

"Yeah." She patted my leg. "You're right."

She was quiet a few minutes, and I took a deep breath and watched the landscape slip by.

I knew about Hope's mom, but frankly I didn't think about her very often, which I felt bad about. Her name had been Sally. She'd gone to Nashville, Tennessee, the summer Hope was six to make some test recordings, demos they're called. She was taking the demos to agents when she was killed in a car wreck.

I twisted in the seat, wishing I could think of something to say.

Hope gave me a quick smile again. "I wish you'd known her, Carin. She was a great mom, just like yours."

Her words made me feel more tongue-tied. "I'm sorry she died."

"Well, it was long before you came along. My 'forever,' you know. Yours is shorter, that's how it goes."

The truth was that Hope and Mom and Dad were always in my life—they were my "forever," as Hope had said. I truly did forget sometimes about Hope's life before Davenport. Her "forever" was ten years longer than mine.

Hope made herself laugh. "Hey, Carin. It could be that for all the trouble cow farts cause, they may be great for radio reception."

I laughed, too, and sank into my seat. We drove on that way, things feeling a little sad and somehow more peaceful, old songs playing behind a layer of static. I thought about Hope's mom and how, if she were alive, we might hear her singing on the radio. If she were alive, though, Dad and my mom wouldn't have married, and there'd be no me.

A truck stacked with wire cages of chickens passed us, and feathers blew across our window.

"Do you suppose this is what it's like to drive around heaven? Angel wings shedding everywhere?" Hope reached forward as if she could touch one through the glass.

"It's pretty, isn't it?" I said.

She glanced at me, and her eyes seemed to be saying a lot that I couldn't understand.

9

We passed all of the exit signs for North Platte—and the Hardee's and the Holiday Inns and the Burger Kings—and I began to believe we truly were heading for the edge of Nebraska.

"You know what, Hope? We just drove into mountain daylight time. It's an hour earlier."

She made her eyes look buggy. "I'll pretend I'm an hour less pooped."

Mileage signs appeared for Ogallala and Kimball. After those towns, I knew, would come Wyoming. I stared off into the thin smudges of clouds. They looked as though they'd been swirled by a giant broom.

Suddenly I smelled something funny—something bad. "Hope, smell that?"

"More cow farts?" She wrinkled her nose. "No, you're right. Something's burning."

"Look!" I pointed at smoke coming out the side of the hood.

"Oh, cripes"—Hope leaned into the dials in front of her—"the heat gauge!"

We were next to the exit for Hershey, so Hope pulled off

and slowed the car way down. We peeked at each other, scared.

Now what, I thought, but I didn't say it aloud. I gave my compass a quick look. We'd turned north.

We crept across the Platte River and into town. Each second the smoke poured harder. Hope slowed to a crawl, pulled to the curb, and turned off the engine. We'd passed one of those IF YOU LIVED IN HERSHEY, YOU'D BE HOME NOW signs. For a second I wished that Dad *did* live in Hershey, Nebraska.

Before we had a chance to start complaining about this old wreck of an Escort, a warm voice at my elbow made me jump.

"Need some help?"

An old woman bent over and smiled at us. Her white hair stuck out from under a small black straw hat that fit her head like a bottle cap. Her teeth looked crackled, and a couple of them had gold along the edge. She wore a dark blue coat. A coat! In this weather.

"You want some help?" she repeated. "Sounds like your engine's taking a rest."

Hope nodded. She looked a little numb, almost speechless for a change. "Yeah, we've got a problem."

The woman stood up and opened my door. "I should say so. You all come along with me. You come to Alma's. I live real close by. We'll get you some lemonade, and then we'll get Hal to take care of the car."

"Hal?" Hope said, dazed. "Maybe we should get Hal first."

"I just live a couple blocks. It's the nearest phone you'll find. Come on now."

I found myself stepping out of the car for this stranger. We locked the doors and Hope propped up the hood. Then she joined the old woman and I followed. They were talking about the heat and about Hershey. I reached up to tighten my barrette and jerked my hand away. "Drat!" A single minute in the sun had already cooked it. I looked at my fingers for blisters. The sun is hotter in Nebraska, I swear. I wondered if it was those cow farts again, acting like a magnifying glass over the whole state, or maybe it was God's revenge for wiping out so many buffalo, not to mention the native tribes. Of course, Nebraskans didn't exactly have an edge on those behaviors.

I hurried to catch up with Hope and the old woman, who was big as a washtub but hustled down the sidewalk like she was in a speed-walking contest. No matter what, I couldn't believe the woman was actually wearing a coat.

I looked back down the street. Our car seemed to be on the edge of the main drag, as main as a street gets in Hershey. Every step I took, the car shrank, smaller and smaller, like a kite being whipped farther away into the sky. We were losing each other, the car and me, and it was the only home I had right now. I hated leaving my stuff there. I could hear this woman saying again and again how Hershey was a great place to live. And I kept trying not to think about that other Nebraska woman, the crazy woman in the newspaper who shot her gun. Did she wear hats like bottle caps and coats in the summer?

"Lemonade," she said, "you girls need lemonade." This was the third time she'd said it. We turned a corner, and I looked back once more to watch the car slip behind some bushes. I hadn't been this far away from the car since Atlantic, and I sure didn't want to lose it again like I had there. The whole idea of a car suddenly seemed imaginary. I was lost.

Alma suddenly led us off the sidewalk toward the skin-niest house I'd ever seen. It looked as if somebody'd had long boards and short boards, and instead of sawing them up to make a square house, they put them together just as they were. The house had a big yard, so it wasn't like there wasn't room for something wider.

I followed Hope and the old woman as they walked up front steps as wide as the house, through the tall doors into her windowless front hall, which at least was a relief from the beating sun. On the left was a long, high staircase that led into darkness. The handrail began with a tall cylinder of smooth wood that looked like the long arm of a dark-skinned dancer, and as I stared at it, I felt pulled up the stairs into whatever was there. I blinked and looked away. The only light was a single bare bulb hanging high above us, and my eyes were still so full of sun that I couldn't see much.

In front of us was a hallway narrowed by stuff piled on both sides. It looked like a tall, narrow tunnel. Hope twist-ed around and looked at me with a big, questioning expression. What a relief! I wasn't in this alone.

Hope followed Alma, and I followed Hope. I wondered

for a second if I'd ever see my mother or father again. I was somewhere I'd never been before, in a stranger's house, and nobody except Hope knew I was there. It was a bad feeling. I moved closer to Hope as we made our way through the hall, and she reached back to find my hand and give it a squeeze.

My eyes were growing used to the dimness as we started down the hall. On one side, newspapers and magazines were piled higher than my head, some tied in bundles, some loose. Any slight earth tremble might bring them down. On the other side were stacks of cardboard boxes—three, four, five high—with crushed and punctured corners that leaked clothing and papers and the yellowed edges of old paperbacks. The air was thick with the smell of an old closet, undisturbed, dead. I sucked in a breath and hoped there was oxygen in it. Surely, I reminded myself, surely this time Hope would know if we were in danger, and she'd take action if it was needed.

We stepped around grocery bags full of empty cans and bottles, a wooden box of old boots, bags of cat litter, and several used-up cushions with dirty edges and foam rubber pushing through. Deep into the hallway, the stacks ended, and there was a small table. In the faint light I could see a plastic bicycle basket leaning against the wall with all kinds of dusty junk in it—a small picture of Jesus, a Halloween witch candle, a Minnie Mouse bank, and a bottle of Jergens hand lotion. All coated in dust. A worn book with gold-edged paper—diary, probably—was jammed into the front. I could imagine that all of the stuff had once been on the top of some girl's dresser—somebody's childhood right there. I pulled my body into the thinnest self possible to keep clear of it. The smell of dirt and must, old papers and clothes, too much stuff sitting for too long—it gagged me. This tunnel was beginning to feel like a doomed mineshaft.

Then I heard the sound of metal sliding on metal as the old woman turned a knob and opened a door. Pushing on Hope, I nearly fell into the fresh air and bright light. There were dozens of square panes in three wide windows. It felt like we were on a porch, but this was the kitchen. The windows let in so much sunshine that I thought for a moment there was no glass. How could this wide, bright, clean room be part of the rest of this skinny house with the jumbled hallway?

"Make yourselves to home," the woman said, taking her hat off and easing her thick arms out of her coat, which looked about as thin as paper. She was wearing a shiny blue dress with white flowers on it, and she had on hose that stopped in rolls at her knees. "I'll hang this up and be right back."

I leaned toward Hope and whispered, "Is that what they call a housecoat?"

The woman heard me and ducked her head back in. "Gracious no, child. A housecoat is what you wear to breakfast. You know. This is my going-uptown coat." She went back into the hall, and I glanced at Hope, who was of course giving me a "shut up" look. Well, that shooting story from the newspaper made me think that *somebody* had to look out for us.

Hope, relaxing now, casually scraped a kitchen chair away from the table and sat down as though this was old territory. I, on the other hand, sat down carefully on a nearby step stool, poised for a getaway. I leaned toward Hope and whispered, "Do you think this is a good idea?"

"Shhh!"

"You girls must be exhausted," Alma said as she came in the kitchen again. She pulled on the long handle of her ancient refrigerator, flicked open the little freezer door inside, and lifted two trays of ice cubes from a shelf along the top. A wave of chilled air slid across my feet. I looked down at them, as though I might see a stripe of frost clinging to me.

The woman reached behind a small floor fan and turned it on. It added a quiet hum to the room and rotated slowly, pushing at the layers of heavy air for a moment before moving on.

"You girls are all aflush from this heat, but I'm making two-tray lemonade. You'll feel better in a lick and a minute." She smiled at us—Hope, then me—as she kept putting things on the counter: a plastic bag of lemons, a big-bellied glass pitcher, and a glass dish with a raised, ridged center for juicing fruit. My mouth started to water. But I kept waiting for the sugar. Could it be that lemonade was different in Nebraska? Sugarless? Was it a better way to fight off the heat? My lips pinched at the thought.

"This is really nice," Hope said.

Turning on the good manners, I thought, but I let it go.

I was too tired to start having rude thoughts. I just wanted the car fixed.

"I saw your Illinois license plate. What part of the state you from? You gals drive all that way today?" She talked in breathy tones as she firmly twisted the lemon halves back and forth on the juicer.

"We left yesterday," Hope said. "From near the Mississippi." I waited for her to ramble on, but she didn't.

In front of one of the many windows was a long, skinny table with seven jars of candy at one end and a wide, clear vase at the other. A single brown and purple iris angled stiffly out of the glass. Around the bottom of the vase, she had left a white furry shawl of some kind. Something else this weird woman wore in the summer heat, I thought.

"Treats, Buttercup, come on," Alma said.

I was totally confused as she put a squeezed lemon on the floor. The white furry shawl moved and then stretched. A big cat yawned, leapt down, and ambled over to lick the leftover lemon pulp. My eyes could have popped out of my head.

Alma scraped the last of the lemon juice into the pitcher, flipped the ice cubes out with a rap-rapping on the counter, and then reached into a canister that I hadn't noticed. Ah, sugar. She poured without measuring and then stirred and stirred the cloudy mixture with a wooden spoon as the cubes clinked away. After I saw sugar added to our drink, I relaxed and stared at the strange cat.

"I used to hate that old cat," Alma said. "She was always

dragging in sweet birds or little mice, dead or nearly dead. I'd scream at her but it didn't help."

"We had a cat like that," Hope said.

Alma continued without a pause. "That's cats, I know, but I didn't like it. You sit down to a plateful of dinner and notice a stray sparrow feather sticking to a kernel of your corn niblets, your whole appetite bites the dust, right? The worst though was this other thing."

I moved to a chair by the table as Alma reached into the cupboard and then poured lemonade into old metal glasses, one maroon, one aqua, one gold. She brought the glasses over and stripes of sweat immediately sprang from the sides. "Now drink up, you girls."

She put white cookies on a plate in front of us. The skin on her hands was so shiny that I wondered if she had any pores left, if skin just flattened out when you got old. Alma herself sat down with a large sigh.

"The worst thing, though," she said, motioning again to the cat, "she had this habit of waking me in the night with her claws—scratching my lips or my nose. Can you imagine? It felt like needle torture. Horrible way to wake up. So I decided to poison her."

I let out a gasp and Alma blinked at me. We both looked at the half-eaten cookie in my hand. She cleared her throat and carried on.

"You know, my own kind of mercy killing, rather than that capital punishment they dish out at the shelters. Save them having to do this one." She hunched her shoulders a little and looked directly at me, and she must have read my mind. "I couldn't give her away with such a terrible habit. What kind of gift is that?" She looked off into space again. "I finally bought some arsenic."

I tried to hold the bite of cookie in one side of my mouth while chewing on air. Maybe then the poison wouldn't spread. But the cookie crumbled inside my cheek, dissolved, and moved around my mouth like soft mud. I imagined the molecules of sugar and arsenic sliding right through the walls of my tiny veins, marching right into my bloodstream and toward my brain. *Stop,* I almost screamed. My hands felt clammy, I began to see flashing lights from the corners of my eyes. I thought I'd faint dead away.

"These are great," Hope said, holding up the last bite of a cookie before tossing it into her mouth. "Real lemony, just like the drink."

I looked at her with my eyes as wide as could be, trying to shout, "No!" But she was looking hard at Alma while she picked up another cookie!

"You know, though, I couldn't do it, couldn't poison the little critter," Alma said.

I felt a rush of relief—like I'd rejoined the living—and swallowed what hadn't already slid down my throat.

"Instead," Alma went on, "I made a voodoo doll out of one of those little stuffed kittens you find in the department stores where the baby clothes are. They had a white one that looked just like her, like my Buttercup."

I looked down at the cat and then out the big windows. I couldn't believe I was sitting across from a woman who wore hose to her knees, saved newspapers and cans to

81

recycle even if she never got around to turning them in, fixed lemonade from scratch, and then made a voodoo doll to kill her cat.

"I hexed her to get run over or to eat some rotten, dead animal—something pretty fast and pain-free, I thought. I was so sure something would work that I bought only one can of cat food at a time. I just knew each one would be the last. I swear, it made me so mad. Each time I'd scoop the last bit of that stinky cat food into her dish, I'd say 'damn' because it meant I probably had to go spend another quarter on another can of cat food. That was a while ago, and that's all cat food cost then."

"Why didn't you have her declawed?" Hope asked.

Alma shook her head and looked at Hope a little sharply. "I couldn't do that. Nobody does that around here, that's for city people." She returned her gaze to her lemonade, touching the fingers of both hands to the glass as if to check the temperature. Hope and I looked at each other, and I thought maybe she was sensing that we might need to hightail it out of here.

"Anyway," she went on, "nothing seemed to be happening, so I took her out on County Highway forty-two, across the interstate. I figured she'd have the good sense to keep heading south to Texas, or if she was fool enough to come north, she'd find a quick, blessed death under the wheel of a Mack truck. I know it sounds mean, but I was getting no sleep. Something had to be done."

Alma took a nibble of cookie herself and washed it down with lemonade before going on.

"But what do you know, she made it back twice, all the way to the house, God knows how, and I tell you there was fire in her eyes both times. She'd sit on the footstool over there"— she motioned to an easy chair with an ottoman in front of it that sat in one corner of the big kitchen—"and curl into one of those lazy cat curlicues like she was sleeping. But if I peeked close, I could see her eyes open a little and darts flying at me, one after the other. Of course, it made me afraid to go to sleep, but I finally would. And more than likely I'd be awakened by her sharp old claws pouncing on my face. She drew blood more than a few times."

I looked at Hope for guidance. We were in the middle of nowhere with a crazy old woman, a cat that attacked people while they slept, a broken car down the road, and nobody—*nobody*—knew we were here.

"So I took what I thought would be the final step. I was picking my sister up at the airport at North Platte, which is about twenty miles to the east. But you know that because you're on the road yourselves. I'd only slept about three hours the night before, because of this feline monster, and I was sick to death of her. I put her in a cardboard box, drove over to the airport, and left the box at the edge of the parking lot. I knew there was a chance some unlucky person might pick her up but at that point, I didn't care. I had to put my trust in fate, like you do sometimes."

I looked at Hope again, waiting for some signal. Nothing.

"My sister and I had a good visit like always. She comes once a year and usually brings me a fancy pillow with some of her latest stitchery on it." Alma took a swallow of lemonade and waved again at the chair in the corner, which we now noticed held two pillows with embroidery on them. I wondered if we were going to get back to the cat story, but Alma didn't seem like a person you should interrupt.

"On that particular visit, she skipped the fancy stuff and brought me one of those funny neck pillows you see in the mail-order catalogs. It's supposed to give you a good rest and prevent your snoring. She'd been using one herself for a while and thought I'd like one. I tried it right away and I slept like a baby, no matter about the snoring, since I live alone. I was hooked, for sure.

"So a week after Sarah leaves, guess what? Old Buttercup strolls onto the porch like it's just another day and meows as sweet as you please. She's clean as I left her and just as plump. I looked at her eyes close-up and there looked to be cannons there aimed at me. She was back, all right. For revenge, I thought.

"I considered locking her out of my room that night, but I hate locked doors, fire you know, and I decided if she attacked me again I'd just take her to the vet and have her put down. But the queer thing was that not even *one single time* did she wake me up. Not once. It was like when she first came to me. Day after day, she curled up on my lap or lay on the couch, meowing quietly now and then but leaving me alone at night. She turned sweet all over again."

Alma took a long drink of her lemonade. "What I figured out finally was that I'd been snoring and she couldn't stand it. She was trying to rip my face out. She was probably trying to save me, you know, get rid of some horrible monster in my head. Who knows? I spoiled her plenty after I realized the situation. So now she's my sweet Buttercup again."

Alma picked up the cat and placed it on her wide lap. Buttercup sank into the space and spread out like gravy. "She even stopped bringing in the wildlife. She got to be real nice, and so here she is. Isn't it funny. Somebody does stuff to you that you think is mean as the devil, but all the time they're doing it 'cause they love you."

"I bet you're glad you didn't kill her," I said, boldly reaching for another cookie.

"Oh, who knows? She was a rotten cat then. No way I could have guessed she'd turn nice. At the time, I'd have been just as happy if she died. Sounds mean, but it's truth. I had no idea, you know."

I was beginning to feel more comfortable with this woman—giving us fresh lemonade and cookies in this heat—but something still made me nervous. It probably wasn't her fault. That story about the shooting made me suspicious of Nebraskans, especially old ladies, and we still had a broken car.

Alma stood then and walked over to the counter, opened one of the drawers, and pulled out a gun. Hope spit her lemonade into the air, and my stomach took off for Spain. Dead at thirteen. Why me? And in this bright, smacking-clean kitchen.

"Look at this," she said, ignoring the expressions on our faces. "It's a shame a person has to keep something like this around, but you just have to anyway."

She held it in her hand like a baby bunny, and I could hear myself panting. It was odd, this war weapon resting in the old woman's hands. I felt like I was living someone else's life.

"You heard about the shooting in Omaha, I suspicion."

She laid the gun on the table, next to the plate of cookies. Talk about a still life. I thought I might even draw a picture when we got back on the road, which seemed like a truly weird thought as soon as I thought it. *If* we ever got back on the road.

"You have it a long time?" Hope asked, sounding like she was asking the price of bananas.

"Not 'til last March," Alma said. "There was a bad murder then. Nothing like what happened yesterday, much more unlucky. You never know when it's going to be you."

"Well, you never know when anything will happen," I said. Hearing myself, I wasn't sure why I'd said it, but if talking would keep me alive a little longer, maybe I should give it a try.

"You're right about that," she agreed.

"Righto!" Hope continued and reached for a third cookie. She held it up. "This cookie could contain the grain of sugar that finally feeds some fat old bacteria that sits on my bicuspid that makes a hole big enough to be a black spot on the X-ray that inspires the dentist to drill an even bigger hole that he has to fill that makes his secretary send me a bill that I have to pay. This cookie at this moment might cost me eighty bucks."

I looked hard at her. She seemed to be losing her mind, right here in Hershey, one heck of a place to be parted with the only thing that you could count on, as Dad liked to say.

I slid my knuckles over the outside of my pocket until I felt the wishbone, and then I pushed on it for whatever luck it might bring.

"You got it," Alma said with a chuckle, which made me jump because for a second I thought she'd read my mind.

"Can we call about the car?" I asked, to see if I had any chance of a future.

"The car," she said, "the car. I clean forgot. So nice having company."

My breath eased a little. It seemed she maybe didn't plan to murder us after all.

Next to the door was a tiny table with an ancient black telephone. Not only did it have a round dial, but its receiver sat crosswise, and whatever it was made of had no shine left at all. I'd seen such phones in old movies, but never in person. Alma dialed, waited, and then talked to someone named Hal, describing the car and the location without missing a beat.

She ended with, "Fifteen minutes? We'll be there."

Hope and I stood, took our glasses to the sink, and rinsed them out. I guess we were so happy to be alive that we'd made instant resolutions about what well-mannered guests we could be.

Alma took the cookie plate away, and the gun was left sitting on the table as the only decoration. A centerpiece,

I thought. *Piece.* I'd heard it called that on TV. Packing a piece. Or was it supposed to be *peace?*

The cat leapt onto the table, circled around the black weapon, and settled herself around it. I couldn't look.

Alma clicked off the fan and went for her hat and coat.

"You don't have to come along," Hope said, when Alma came back to the kitchen. I wanted Alma to stay, too, to protect her cat and her gun. I was trying to appreciate her kindness, but I still felt uneasy.

"No trouble. I'll come along."

She picked up the gun again and my heart twitched.

"Best put this away before someone gets hurt. I hate having to own it." She slipped it back into the drawer and eased it shut. My heart returned to its rightful place and began slowing down.

I couldn't wait to get back on the road, and I held my sweating fingers crossed all the way to the car for good luck, which we were badly in need of.

10

Hal had his head under the hood when we got there. "Alma, you got the best scented perfume in town," he said even before he pulled his head out. "I could smell you coming a half block away."

Hal wore the cleanest overalls I'd ever seen on a mechanic. In fact, he was altogether clean—even his hands looked like they hadn't touched grease until this very minute. His thin brown and gray hair was parted straight and combed neatly, and smile wrinkles flagged his eyes.

Alma's face flushed. I'd never seen an old person blush, and it made me suddenly feel happy and carefree. And safe.

He stood up, eased the grease off onto a faded red rag, and smiled at us. "Things don't look too bad. A couple of belts, some fluid, I'll adjust a few other things. You gals were pretty lucky, I think, especially lucky that Alma spotted you." For the moment, everything seemed as good as it could be.

"So will it take long to fix?"

"Not long at all. I'll go to the station, fetch what I need, and be back shortly." He turned to Alma with a question in his wrinkled forehead. "You let me give you a ride home, Alma. Out of this heat."

"But the girls." She motioned to us with a worried expression.

He looked at us with a playful grin. "They look like a pair that can take care of themselves." He turned back to Alma. "Besides, if you come with me, my truck'll have the best-smelling cab in the state. At least for a couple of hours."

Her eyelids actually seemed to flutter shyly. "And you girls'll take care of each other then?"

We nodded.

"You be sure to call me if anything comes up. I'm happy to help. Alma Peabody in Hershey. You call, you hear?" She pulled a couple of Hershey kisses out of her coat pocket, held them out like prizes, and handed us each one. I dangled mine by its paper strip, the same way I'd held a tiny lizard up by its tail once at camp.

"We will," Hope said agreeably. "You've been a huge help. Thanks."

"Yeah, thanks a lot," I said.

She nodded then and let Hal boost her into the cab of his pickup. We stood there and watched them drive away the same as Mom had stood and watched us head out of her yard into the rest of the country.

"Isn't it great how nice people can be," Hope said as she watched them drive off.

I nodded. "Yeah. If only you could tell in advance."

She perked up her eyebrows in agreement.

———

Soon we were again heading west on Interstate 80, poorer by seventy-eight dollars, but we had a new fan belt tightly in place that was spinning things along. And whatever else needed fixing was fixed. I remembered my fear about car trouble when Mom had given me the just-in-case money. Now we'd had it, and I felt better. It was a relief to be on the highway in a freshly repaired car.

I pulled out the atlas again. "You know, Hope, if you took Interstate 76 into Colorado, we'd nearly be out of Nebraska now."

She glanced at me with a smile at the edge of her lips. "I'd think you'd see such a plan as cheating."

I shrugged. "We'll still get to Nevada."

"Let's stay on 80. There's no way to get lost. I thought you'd like that."

"Yeah. I like that."

We drove on in a happy silence for a while. We ate our Hershey's Kisses cap, and I used another miniature clip to attach the little white streamers with the word KISSES on them to the clothesline that decorated our ceiling. The afternoon sun reflected on the pavement in front of us like a long tongue of fire. Hope seemed to be staring it down as she drove. Her face grew tight and her arms, tense. When we passed Ogallala, she finally spoke. "How many miles are *in* Nebraska?"

Glad to have something to do, I found all the tiny triangle mileage markers on the map, wrote down the numbers between each pair, and added them up. "Four hundred seventy-nine," I said finally.

Hope let out a big sigh. "If the fan belt hadn't gone, we'd nearly be done." She seemed to be talking to herself. The stop had ended up taking more than two hours. "Hungry?" she asked.

"A little. You know, Hope, I don't really care if we get all the way across tonight. We're so close. And you started driving in Iowa, after all." She deserved some praise.

"Well, sometimes I've gone seven hundred in a day, so this seems cinch-y."

"But we had car trouble."

She was lost in her thoughts. "Heck, Carin, doesn't a dip in a pool sound great?"

"Yes!" I pulled at my T-shirt to lift it away from my skin for a minute. "Absolutely. Even another car wash would feel good."

We watched for billboards and soon saw an advertisement for the Happy Trails Motel in Sidney with a pool and rooms starting at forty-nine dollars.

I did some more calculations. "If we stay at Sidney, we'll only have sixty miles in the morning until we're out of Nebraska."

"Great. How about we do it before breakfast—just like the nutty parents used to do."

I smiled. "As long as we don't have to leave at seven or some other Parent Hour."

I pulled out the yellow Whitman Sampler box again and chewed more gum to add to my relief map, pressing the black highway thread down into the fresh sticky goo with a pencil. The map now reached beyond Nebraska into the beginnings of Wyoming.

Outside the Happy Trails Motel stood a life-size plastic horse. I felt like we'd entered another country. And, of course, there was a vacancy. Sidney was not like some big vacation spot.

We unloaded our stuff and walked to a little café a half block away. They had a pay phone, so I called Mom. As I dialed all the numbers, I felt my stomach go sort of wavy. Nobody home. I took a deep breath while my voice played on the answering machine, and I left a quick message. At least now she wouldn't have to worry.

I ate a hamburger and fries, and Hope had some noodle special that she said seemed to be flavored with Mystery Meat Number Nine. I suddenly wanted to ask her why she was being so much nicer today than she had been yesterday, but I thought better of it. Maybe I was being nicer, too, and I didn't know if it would last. I wasn't sure I could trust things. I mean, just a short while ago we'd been eating cookies and drinking lemonade with a woman who kept a gun in her kitchen. Maybe it was common in Nebraska, but it wasn't common in my life. I needed to stay alert.

We swam until the pool closed and then collapsed—we *each* had a bed. Unbelievable.

In the morning, I woke up to something tickling the bottom of my feet. "Hey!"

Hope was standing at the end of the bed in her swimsuit. From her fist peeked a wadded-up tissue she was using on my toes. I lunged at her.

She laughed. "Come on, let's go for a dip before another day in the oven."

Before we left the motel, Hope made me stand by the plastic horse for a photo.

"Do you think it'll look real in the picture?" I said.

"I bet it will."

The dip in the pool felt great, but it made me hungry, too. I looked at the map. "So is Kimball the breakfast stop?"

She nodded. "And the last stop in Nebraska."

Before I knew it, we were sliding into a booth at the highway restaurant.

"You gals look mighty hungry," the waitress said with a wide smile. She was tall and had a big gap between her two front teeth, and she was wearing about fifteen tiny pins on her uniform—all kinds of fish and turtles.

"You?" Hope looked at me.

I was staring at a large picture of exactly what I wanted. "A big waffle with strawberries and whipped cream, please. And orange juice."

"You're starting to eat like a truck driver," my sister said.

"I feel like a truck driver."

The waitress wrote down my order. "Being on the road—it makes a gal hungry, hungry. That's what I always say."

Hope ordered eggs, toast, and a large coffee. I watched as she opened her wallet under the table. I figured she was counting up. She suddenly looked up. "Okay, what's today's plan? Wyoming?"

"It's another twenty miles to the state border." I'd already done some homework. "And then it's 401 through Wyoming."

"So we should—*barring disaster*—we should easily be able to sleep in Utah."

"Utah tonight," I repeated, lifting my water glass high.

We ate quickly and hit the road again. No more messing around. We had someplace to go, and we had to *get* there.

11

There's nothing like a waffle loaded with strawberries and whipped cream to bring on a good snooze. When I woke, we were about an hour into Wyoming, passing the last exit for Cheyenne and another sign, LARAMIE 46.

Suddenly I gasped.

"What!" screamed Hope. "What?"

"Sorry. I thought it was a dead calf or something. A pile of hay, I guess."

Hope put her hand on her chest. "My heart. Please."

I pulled out my notebook and map to figure out how our trip was coming. For some reason, the numbers helped me. I wrote down

Distance from Davenport—740 miles
Distance to Reno—1,023 miles

and put the book away. I kept hoping we'd be halfway, but that was still hours away.

A station wagon filled with kids in the back passed us, and all of them pressed their little faces against the glass so they looked like a row of dried apricots. Then they pulled back and laughed and waved. We waved and laughed with them.

After Laramie, we pulled into a rest stop, did what we needed to do, and zipped right back on the road.

"Let's have a real stop in Rawlins. That'll be about two hundred miles so far today, and I need a stretch," Hope said, fingering her jade necklace again.

"I want to call Mom, too, to try to get her in person."

"Yes, we don't want the parents to worry."

"Wish I could drive," I said for the second time.

"Me, too."

My ears nearly fell off my head. Of all the kind things Hope had said to me, I thought this one was the nicest ever.

We parked near downtown in Rawlins, and after lunch we headed across the street to a St. Vincent de Paul store of secondhand stuff. "A little adventure?" she said and cocked her eyebrows.

The building must have been a warehouse at one time. There were huge double doors and a cement floor. We strolled past rows of couches—some with wooden armrests and some with little skirts around the bottom, plaid, plain, or decorated with large splotchy flowers. Most of them looked like they'd been sat on and sprawled over a good bit. Stuffed chairs—with flat or fat cushions—were crowded together in the next rows. Then came tables: side tables, end tables, coffee tables, and kitchen tables with chairs turned upside down on their tops. The place smelled a little musty, of course, like old stuff and dirty concrete, but it felt good to walk around and be out of the car. Lots of other shoppers were browsing, too.

Racks of clothes followed. Then we came to shelves and tables of kitchen appliances, dishes, utensils, tools, books, and more. Here and there, fans hummed busily and blew a little air around to make us think we were a little cooler than we were.

"It's not like we have that much room in the car," I reminded her as she eyed a lamp that was about as tall as a giraffe.

"Hey, look!" She ignored me and headed for a table with carnival junk, swooping down on those goofy plastic sunglasses, the kind that are twice as wide as your head. "We've *got* to get these! Here."

She plucked a pair with purple and green swirls for herself and held out orange- and pink-striped ones for me. I snatched them, and we mugged for each other, which made us keel over laughing.

We moved on, picking up this and that, potato ricers, vegetable peelers, muffin pans, and candleholders. A little burp of sound—"OH"—suddenly popped out of Hope.

She reached under a table and came up gripping an object that made my heart sink—the top half of a mannequin. "How cool is this!" The look on Hope's face said it all.

"That wasn't a real question, was it?"

She was puckering her lips and thinking. "Wow, Carin. This is a find."

I tried to imagine it with a wig and the bottom half of itself. "I'm telling you it's weird. How much?"

"Eight," she said in a hushed tone, as if someone might triple the price if they heard her say it out loud. "I could really use this, you know?"

"Do you think it'll fit in the car?"

"It'll fit. Somehow."

I had some doubts about having a stiff-armed mannequin top in the car, but Hope was so happy. I suddenly wanted to find something wonderful, too, and I turned back down the aisle, with my eyes sailing up and down the shelves the way a hawk circles round, scouring the land for some poor dumb mouse. *Look! Look harder!* I kept saying to myself, wanting desperately to bring my gaze in for a landing on the ultimate and perfect thing.

Then it happened. I rounded a rack of recipe books and there sat an entire shelf of waffle makers. I loved waffle makers even more than I loved waffles. They had solid weight and a clear purpose. If a waffle maker were a car, it would be a yellow taxi, and if it were a coat, it could withstand Arctic winters. Strong and solid.

Most of the waffle irons on the shelf looked okay but rather ordinary. I poked around a little because some were piled two layers thick, and then I found it—one that was truly unusual. Instead of a single square or circle, this one had two separate small, square irons sitting on one rectangular metal tray. Wow. The chrome had some black spots, but maybe they'd scrub off. And only six dollars. I picked it up; it weighed a ton, which is precisely how much waffle irons should weigh.

"Very nice." Hope was standing a few feet away. I'd been so lost in my waffle dreams that I hadn't noticed her.

"It won't take up much room in the car," I said, suddenly fearing that she'd be mad.

"It's great. It'll be fine—easier than Mildred here."

I smiled at Mildred, then at Hope, suddenly feeling as if Hope and I were in on something together. "She'll fit next to the cooler," I said. "I'm sure of it."

We were headed toward the checkout when I saw some clocks on the wall. One of them was like some of Mom's clocks, with old-fashioned big numbers, but it was in a triangular pale green case. She didn't have anything like that.

"Look, Hope."

I set my stuff down and went to the clock. Only four dollars and fifty cents. What a bargain.

"Excellent!" she said with a smile. "Clock and waffle iron. How kitcheny."

"Kitschy?" I said and poked her in the ribs.

We paid and headed out. As we approached the car, we could see a small white paper tucked under the windshield wiper. "Darn!" said Hope.

She snatched what turned out to be an envelope, a parking ticket, looked at it for a minute, and burst out laughing. "Listen to this. It has a red message stamped over the parking fine. 'Welcome to Rawlins. Don't worry about the expired parking meter. We're happy to have you stopping by our city. We hope you have a good time.' Is that great or what?"

"Why doesn't Iowa do that?"

"We have to add this to our souvenir line," Hope said, handing me the nonparking ticket. When she unlocked the door, it took us about a minute to see that the mannequin wouldn't go into the backseat at all, let alone fit next to the cooler. Her arms bent only up and down, they wouldn't tuck in close.

"If only I were teeny-weeny, then I could sit by the food and it could sit in front," I said.

"Thank you. That's a generous offer."

"What should we do?" I already felt a certain fondness for the odd thing.

"I see only one solution. The roof."

"Hmm?"

"We'll need something to pad it."

"There was a bin of blankets at St. Vincent's. I'll get one."

"Great. I think there's rope in back."

The waffle iron and clock fit easily on the floor behind my seat. I went back for a blanket and spotted a tray filled with bottles of bubbles. How had we missed those? I bought two.

When I returned, Hope was untangling an orange rope. I tucked the bubbles into my backpack to surprise her later and spread the old brown blanket over the roof of the car.

A few people walking by smiled at us. Perhaps watching two people preparing half a mannequin for the roof of a car is a fun thing to see on a Thursday afternoon.

Hope began weaving the rope around Mildred's neck and under her arms.

"The trick is not to wind the rope around her neck," I said. "Too scary."

"There's that, Sis," Hope sighed. I found I didn't mind it so much that she called me Sis.

She set the mannequin on the roof and coiled the rope around and under her arms. Very quickly, we both saw how far the ends would go—or *not* go. The rope was too short. "Drat!"

"We need a better plan." She lifted Mildred off the roof, and we started unwinding the rope when a man's voice made us both turn.

"WEST WITH HOPELESS," he read in a slow drawl, pointing at the sign. "Sounds like trouble. You gals need a little help?"

Another helpful stranger? I didn't know if I could stand it. For a second, I wondered if Alma Peabody from Hershey, Nebraska, had put out an all-points bulletin on us.

Hope nodded. "I guess what we need are directions to the nearest hardware store, so I can buy some rope."

The man smiled, and we all stood there and looked at each other for a minute. He was a shiny man and I wished I had my sunglasses on.

He wore shiny brown cowboy boots with swirls carved on the toes, shiny brown pants, and a wide belt with a shiny silver buckle engraved with a bucking bronco. His cowboy shirt had square pearl buttons and those fancy embroidered points on the chest, and, lastly, a shiny turquoise and silver clasp held his string tie in place. The guy practically twinkled. He would definitely have looked at home next to the plastic horse at the Happy Trails Motel. I wondered why he didn't have a cowboy hat to top things off and protect his shiny head.

"No need for a hardware store. I can help you ladies out." With that, he brought his hand around from behind him—aha—and set his cowboy hat on his head. What next? A six-shooter? A guitar? A lonesome doggie tune?

He nodded across the street at Lawson's Real Estate. "Name's Chuck Lawson, and I've got plenty of rope I can let you have. Come on."

"Thanks," Hope said and leaned the mannequin against the car. She whispered to me as we followed him, "What is it about this town? You'd think it was running for a Miss Congeniality prize."

Chuck led us through the front offices and opened a door that led into a large dark warehouse.

"Come on this way," Chuck said. "I've got a collection I want to show you. It won't take long."

Collection of what, I thought. Maybe this wasn't such a great idea. I stood back a little, ready to bolt if things got shady. As Hope stepped through the doorway, she seized my hand and gasped. Before I could flee she pulled me in and then I gasped, too.

Stretched out before us was an astonishing, almost magical sight. Ten, twelve, or more old Volkswagen campers and microbuses were lined up, gleaming even in the dim warehouse light. Greens and yellows and reds. We walked slowly down the line of them, looking at each other once in a while and laughing in relief and amazement at this surprise. I'd never gawked so hard in my life. What a time warp.

Chuck followed along, chuckling. "Quite the sight, isn't it?"

We stopped, overwhelmed I guess, and Chuck led the way to one and then another, opening and closing doors, showing us the restored upholstery, fresh carpets, and cleaned engines.

I could hardly *wait* to tell Mom and Dad about this stop.

"My best friend, Brad, got drafted and asked me to store his bus while he was in Vietnam. It's that one right there," Chuck said, pointing to a white one. "He was killed in the war." He pinched his lips together tightly for a minute. It made me think that he still missed him. Chuck motioned to the van. "His parents wanted me to keep it, and that's how it began.

"Every time I heard about one being for sale, I couldn't resist. I guess that's how collections happen. Well, nostalgia being what it is, it didn't take a brain surgeon to figure out some years back that these honeys would be worth lots of cash at some point. So I grew earnest in my search and bought the last dozen here as fast as I could find them. I've restored them as I have time. They'll be my retirement. Some folks have bonds or stocks, but I'll sell one of these every once in a while to some hippie-type former guru-follower-turned-banker, and I'm in the comfort zone. I've already taken a couple of down payments."

We'd made it to the last bus, which was still a disaster—a milky blue with lots of rust and missing pieces. I opened the passenger door, and saw paper cups, a crushed Kleenex box, bottle caps, wadded-up paper, and lots of dirt on the floor. Hanging from the rearview mirror was a necklace with a peace-sign medallion.

"Look, Hope, real love beads."

Chuck reached around me, and I thought I smelled Ivory soap.

"Here, you girls take this—a souvenir from Chuck's showroom."

As he talked, he worked the string of beads off the mirror and then dropped it into my hands.

"Thanks."

"Wow, this is so cool." Hope looked up and down the row. "I wasn't even alive when they made these things, but I'd love to own one some day."

"Gal, you never know."

He led us back toward the office and paused by a workbench where he lifted a coil of rope from a hook on a wall. He flopped it down and pulled out a knife with a blade that looked suitable for skinning a large animal. I took a step back toward the door—I couldn't help it—as he neatly sliced through the rope. Then he replaced the coil and handed the piece to Hope, who thanked him over and over.

"Wait now," he said, as he fished out his wallet. "Here's a card. You keep in touch, now." He winked at Hope, which I didn't like much. "Better start deciding if it's a green one you want, or maybe red."

Chuck looked down the row of cars with the glow of a jeweler admiring a case of shiny rings. Then he put his finger to his lips. "'Course I'd give the whole thing up in a minute to have Brad back." He took a big breath and slapped his chest. "Well, I've held you gals up long enough. You be sure to keep Chuck's place in mind now."

"I'll start that savings account next week," Hope said, telling a lie as big as his warehouse, and took the card. "Thanks a lot. Thanks a whole lot."

"I'd better come along and make sure it's long enough this time."

The three of us walked back to the car, and I tried to calm my jumping insides.

The rope from Chuck was so long that we easily wrapped it around Mildred, under her arms and back around, through the inside of the car and out again, securing the mannequin safely on the roof. Our unusual cargo seemed as secure as it could be. He helped us by tying some fancy knot.

"Looks great," he said. "You'll have to check the blanket once in a while, but I think it'll stay put," he added slowly. "See if the door closes."

Hope gave it a good slam and the latch clicked shut.

"I think it's another photo op," Hope said, fumbling in back for her camera. "Here." She handed it to Chuck. "Do you mind?"

"Happy to oblige."

We stood by the car, and I held out my compass for effect. He snapped a shot, and then I snapped one of Hope and him.

"Ready to go?" Hope said. I'd already hopped into my seat. I let her take care of the good-byes.

"What a sight those VWs were, huh?" Hope said, still dazed.

I pinned the business card on the tiny clothesline that ran across the ceiling, and wound the beads around the mirror. Hope held the key in the ignition, but she didn't start the car.

"What's wrong?"

"Nothing. All of that was just so amazing. You know, Chuck wouldn't collect VWs if Brad hadn't died." She turned the key. "I guess I'm not the only one who never gets over some things."

I'd never thought about how people were so connected to each other. Nothing had happened to me that *made* me think about it. "All these stories—all these *histories,* Hope, and you can't tell a thing by looking at people."

"Lots of forevers out there. You just never know," she said dreamily and then turned to me with a quick smile. "Hey, how's the food situation? Should we stop at a grocery store?"

I turned around and pawed through the sacks. "Two bags of rice cakes, half a jar of Skippy's, napkins and plastic forks. A can of tuna. Three apples. Also, one dead banana."

"Your mother's right. On the road we eat like starving jackals."

I pulled out the blackened, soft banana and made a face. "It's leaking."

Hope took it from me carefully, as though she were

holding some filthy shoe by its worn-out tongue. "Whoa baby! That bit of vegetation must have gotten some direct sun. Barf-o-Rama." She tossed it through her open window onto the parkway. "Don't worry. By sunset, that little item will be halfway to dirt."

I cocked my eyebrow at her. "You sure you don't see it as a souvenir?'

"Very funny."

"Well, we're definitely down to the dregs. Even including the protein."

"Let's think this through." She held out her fingers and touched each one as she listed meals. "Dinner tonight. Tomorrow, all three, I suppose. Hmmm. Four. And then breakfast Saturday morning."

"After the waffle iron and clock, I have twenty-two dollars left," I offered.

"You can help then. I'm still in pretty good shape. Let's get some fruit and juice at least. Maybe some deli turkey for dinner."

She started the engine and drove until we reached a grocery store.

"And chips. I'll get them. Hey, Hope, can I get a copy of that picture?"

"Cowboy Lawson?"

"No, silly. Us. I don't have a picture of us on my dresser at Mom's." We headed for the door.

Hope gave me a quick, sweet smile.

Inside, I spotted a pay phone and headed for it.

"Say hi for me," Hope called after me. "Tell her I'll call Dad."

I punched all the numbers for the phone card Mom had given me and finally heard a ringing.

"Hello?"

"Mom?"

"Carin! Hello, sweetie, how are you? Where are you? I've tried not to worry, but I'm sure glad you called. I got your message."

I unexpectedly felt a small lump climb into my throat, and I realized how far away I suddenly felt. "Mom?" I said again.

"Is everything all right?"

"It's fine, Mom. Fine." I coughed once. "I just wanted to tell you how fine things are. They're fine."

She laughed. "Good."

"We're in Rawlins, and Hope just bought half a mannequin, and some nice cowboy real estate guy gave us a bunch of rope to tie it on top of the car."

Mom gave a little laugh. "A mannequin? A nice stranger? So everything's all right?"

"Right."

"I'm plotting your trip on the map here, so I'll move the pin along. Your money's holding out?"

"Seems to be."

"Are you having some adventures with your sister?"

A whole bunch of things suddenly came to mind—the weird Laundromat stop, the high school reunion, Alma and her cat and her gun. "We're having a few," I offered, "but we're fine, just fine." We were okay, and that's what she wanted to know.

"So you think you'll arrive by noon Saturday? I'll call your dad and tell him. I'm off work the rest of the week, so I'll be here if you need anything. Okay?"

"Thanks, Mom. Hope said she'd call Dad, too."

"Okay then. Love you, honey."

"Love you, too, Mom."

"Say hi to Hope. And be careful, you two."

We hung up and I went in search of chips, blinking my eyes fast a few times. The call made me feel reconnected. The strings of that triangle I'd imagined as we pulled out of the alley, the one where Mom was the point staying put and Hope and I were the points driving away, and the ribbon of pavement that was Interstate 80 that I'd watched grow thinner and thinner as we'd headed west all seemed strengthened into some kind of harness that I could tug on if I needed to. It made me feel less lost. I was traveling almost on my own, and I was doing pretty well, but I could go back if I wanted.

12

I **put** our food in back while Hope adjusted Mildred. "Carin, we need a new sign."

I stood up and looked at her around Mildred's chin. "Yeah?"

She tugged Mildred's shirt up a little. "RENO OR BUST."

I didn't get it right way, but I chuckled, and then I got it and laughed.

Hope opened the cooler, scooped out water with a plastic cup, and hurled it to the pavement. When she dumped in the new bag of ice, a cloud of cool air hung in the car for a moment. The bottles of juice and plastic bags of fruit sat catty-wampus in the cubes like toys stuck in sand. The fresh bag of ice between us sent out waves of coolness, too. I taped up our nonparking ticket by the rearview mirror. It was too big to hang from the mini-clothesline. Our shrine of travel souvenirs was growing.

I plunged my tennis-wrist cuff deep into the chest of cubes and icy water and pulled it up to my knee. It was so cold I sucked in my breath.

"Good idea there," Hope said.

Jenna's bracelet was finished, so I pulled out my bag of

threads and chose some different colors to start a new one.

"Dad had some news for me about the interview."

"Is everything still on?" I asked.

"Oh, it's on all right. It's more *on* than it used to be?"

"How so?"

"The head honcho's going to Hong Kong on Saturday, and two other people want the job." She turned to look at me. "Did I already tell you this?"

I shook my head, remembering only one nasty and short conversation about Hope's job designing costumes for casino showgirls.

"Dad showed her my photos and sketches, and she said I'd be her top choice, but she wanted to meet me, of course."

"So? Is Saturday still okay?"

"Her flight's been changed to early morning, so she needs to see me Friday night."

"Friday. That's tomorrow." *Tomorrow!* Could we make it? *Impossible,* I thought.

Hope cocked her mouth and nodded. "And we're in Wyoming. We've got to haul some metal big time."

"What would your job there be, exactly?" I was feeling bad about jumping on her earlier.

"Well, I'm not entirely sure, but you know those wonderful sparkly outfits, the wild headpieces—working on all of that, I imagine. And you work with the best fabrics, too; they have to withstand a lot of dancing and constant cleaning."

"Sounds like fun."

She smiled at me. "I think so. If we get there in time."

Wyoming, Utah, clear across Nevada. I pulled out my notebook and map again to do more figuring.

"How late can you see her?"

"She's at the club 'til all hours. If I get there by nine or ten, it'll be fine, she said."

"That helps. But we've got to get to Dad's first for dinner, and you have to clean up"—I interrupted myself and laughed—"nothing personal."

"Yeah. Neither one of us is exactly fit for public appearance, dearie."

"I sure hope the car doesn't break again."

Hope put her fingers to her pursed lips. "Shhhh."

I made my calculations and wrote them down.

Distance from Davenport—949 miles
Distance to Reno—814 miles

"We're over halfway, Hope."

"About time, huh? How much is left?"

"Eight hundred fourteen."

"Well, that's not too bad," she said quietly.

The car clock said nearly two. Traffic was light, and we drove along, nibbling our way through lunch and keeping to ourselves. The towns we passed had great names: Red Desert, Table Rock, Bitter Creek, Point of Rocks. I chewed some gum for a while and reached for the yellow candy box to add to my growing miniature landscape. I added a small chunk a little south of my highway of gum and tweaked it into a point to make Separation Peak.

"Look, Hope," I said, pointing to the mountain. "It's 8,540 feet above sea level."

She smiled. "Just think how short it would look if you were flying over it."

She was right about that. I started chewing one more piece and while it softened and grew sticky, I caught up on my county list. Wyoming had hardly any counties. I couldn't believe it. We'd gone through Laramie, Albany, Carbon, and we were in Sweetwater, which was huge, maybe bigger than Rhode Island. There was only one more, Uinta, and then Wyoming was over. In the back of the atlas, I counted a total of twenty-three counties for the whole state.

"Hey, look," Hope said, pointing out her window. "How cool is that?"

A limousine with four regular bikes and a tandem one on a roof rack was passing us. Hope waved, and a girl in the backseat flapped her hands back at us really hard, pointed at the mannequin, and laughed. Their license plate said 4 BIKRS.

The limo pulled ahead, and we ourselves pressed on.

"Hey, Hope, kids here are lucky," I said, pushing gum into the box.

"Why?" Hope was back in her driving daze.

"Wyoming kids only have to memorize twenty-three counties when they do state history."

"No way."

"Remember Mrs. Wolfnose and the ninety-nine Iowa counties?"

"Wolfson, you mean?"

"Wolfnose. Remember? Because she flared her nostrils every time she was about to get mad."

Hope smiled.

"You made up some ditty using the ninety-nine first letters to help me remember. Remember?"

"Gosh, that was forever ago. Do you still know it?"

"No way. But I did. My friends thought I was so lucky to have such a smart big sister." I thought so, too, I remembered.

Hope looked kind of dreamy. "I'd forgotten that." She looked at me. "That one is part of *our* forever."

That was a nice thing to say, but I hoped she wouldn't make a big deal out of it.

I chattered away for a while. "You know that Sweetwater County we're in, which by the way has a town called Bitter Creek—sweet water, bitter creek, go figure—well, this county looks so big I thought to myself that Rhode Island would probably fit in it. Then I thought people were always saying how little Rhode Island is, and it must be a drag for Rhode Islanders to hear that kind of stuff like it's a drag to always hear people say stupid things about Iowa because people don't know anything about it except that it's somewhere between the East Coast and the West Coast and they think we're all farmers and they think farmers are dumb. Well, so I looked in the atlas. And it turns out that Rhode Island has only 1,545 square miles, so it really is tiny. Wyoming has 97,814. Iowa, by the way, has 55,869."

"Thank you, Dr. Geography. Was there some preaching about Iowa there?"

"Well, I guess. You can't compare something like size with how people act or think. Isn't that true? You know, Mom told me some men did that. They looked at brain size and thought it meant something about how smart people are. Isn't that dumb? If it were totally true, then all adults would be smarter than all kids. Yeah, right."

"Could I have some grapes?"

I gave her some and we drove on. After a while, I pulled up the bottles of bubbles.

"Hey, Hope. Look."

"Bubbles! You goddess!"

I unscrewed the top and handed her one of the bottles.

We blew bubbles out the window mile after mile, surprising the travelers we passed, including a couple in a red car with JUST MARRIED all over the car in white paint. We bubbled our way past Rock Springs. By the time we'd drained the bottles and stopped for a little lunch, we were over a hundred miles closer to the Utah border. Not super close, but not bad.

Hope raised her finger to point at a mileage sign, as we pulled around Green River. "Little America's thirteen miles away."

"Weird name for a town."

She looked at me with a grape half out of her mouth, so her expression had a purple knob in the middle. She sucked it in and chomped it.

"These grapes are good, but I have a hankerin' for some candy."

"'Hankerin'? Did you say 'hankerin'?"

"Whoa, baby, we're out west." She twirled her fingers in a small circle. "Just tryin' to get in the mood."

"Whoa, baby?" I repeated.

"I picked that up in Chicago from a guy who grew up in Maine!"

"You're kidding, right?"

Hope shrugged. "Look"—she pointed—"candy heaven."

I suddenly realized Hope was pulling off on the Little America exit and heading straight for a Wal-Mart.

"Wouldn't you know a town called Little America would have a Wal-Mart. We never go in Davenport. Mom hates Wal-Mart. She likes to say Wal-Mart—where you open your WALlet and your money MARTches right out.'"

"All those bargains?"

"So much junk?"

"You better not tell her about this stop then." Hope pulled into the crowded parking lot and, after a few slow cruisings up and down the lanes, found an empty space.

At the entrance, people milled around as though it were the end of a church service. I didn't know who was coming and who was going, who was shopping and who was not.

One little girl jumped up and down and pulled on her mother's blouse, whining for something. The mother was speaking to another woman who was holding a baby. Both women acted as though they couldn't hear the kid. Actually, I couldn't hear the kid much myself. Her noise seemed to be drowned out by—what—I didn't know. The store was full of the sounds of shopping. Cash registers, carts being wheeled along, people talking or dropping stuff in their carts, and all that noise bouncing off the ceiling.

A young blond woman with KRISTAL on her Wal-Mart name tag greeted us and offered us a cart. But maybe she wasn't offering it to us. People were in front of us and behind us.

When we pushed through the congestion, Hope must have turned on a sugar magnet in her brain. She zeroed in on a distant twirling rack hung like a Christmas tree with bags of candy.

I followed along behind Hope and nearly bumped into a man with a cane, which made me feel stupid, so I veered toward the row of laundry baskets.

"Hey," Hope called after me, "I've got to get some film." She pointed in the direction she was already going and disappeared.

The air conditioning felt good, and when I was farther down the aisle, where it was quieter, I even noticed some piped-in music—some jingly version of an Elton John song. It was a song on one of Mom's tapes.

When I reached the end of the aisle, I headed down the next one. All at once I saw myself reflected in mixing bowls and stainless steel cooking pots. One quart, two quart, stew, frying, large and small. Each one took my face and held it like a wraparound decoration. I was a wide pot, a narrow pot, a flat pot. I was a star. I wondered if this was how famous people felt when they saw themselves on lunch boxes and thermoses and school binders. A whole aisle of yourself staring back at you. Every face was yours. Wal-Mart was beginning to feel like a scary fun house.

I wondered if all Wal-Marts looked alike, with their high ceilings like St. Vincent's in Rawlins. I supposed there were Wal-Marts in Topeka and Cincinnati and Pensacola and Fargo. Lost in Wal-Mart could be big. Even with all of those stretched or shrunken versions of *my* face staring back at my own eyes, I had no way of knowing for sure where I was.

I looked around and wondered where Hope was. Just somewhere in Wal-Mart, I guessed, like me. If we were lost, it could last a long time, but at least we were lost in the same place. That idea made me feel less lost. And if someone came by who worked here, they wouldn't think I was lost at all. As far as they were concerned, I was shopping. Just another kid wandering the aisles in small appliances.

A girl about Hope's age, in one of those tie-at-the-waist vests, came whipping down the aisle, stopped near me to study the irons on the top shelf, muttering all the while, "Automatic off, safety cord, self-cleaning, white handle. Automatic off, safety cord, self-cleaning, white handle," over and over.

She had bad hair and a couple of zits on her chin, and she looked a little scared, like somebody was waiting for her to screw up so they could fire her. I wanted to ask her about a drinking fountain, but I was afraid it might confuse her, and I didn't want to get her in trouble over me.

She zoomed in on what she was looking for and then added the price to her list. She threw me a lippy smile as she turned to go back down the aisle.

I slid to the cool floor, crossed my legs, and suddenly thought of good old Ramona Quimby. I used to take one of those books with me every year on the plane; even after I'd outgrown them, I'd always think of her when I went west. Now I imagined her plopped in the middle of Wal-Mart waiting for her sister. What would she do? She'd either be crabby or she'd make the best of it. I thought about making the best of it. Then it hit me that if I ignored being lost, it wouldn't be true. I was *somewhere,* after all. Maybe even somewhere where snakes brought good luck.

Suddenly there was an announcement on a loudspeaker that drowned out old Elton John. "I'd like to dedicate this next song to the citizens of Little America." I jumped up and looked at the toaster right in front of me. The me that looked back had eyes wide open and a big crinkly smile.

The voice coming through the air was Hope's; she was belting out "The Star-Spangled Banner." I headed up one aisle and down another looking for her.

People had stopped shopping. They cocked their heads at the song to make sure it was actually what they thought it was, and some of them stood with their hands over their hearts.

Two more aisles down, I spotted her standing on a platform under a big ELECTRONICS sign where a karaoke machine was set up. When she saw me, she motioned hard for me to join her. What the heck. I was the better sopra-no, and she was close to the end—she needed me.

" . . . banner yet wave," we sang, and Hope went right to the harmony. "O'er the land of the free." I held this note long and went up a fifth to really make a scene. We slapped our hands together and finished. "And the ho-ome of the brave."

We heard cheers and whistles from all over the store.

"I knew you'd come," she said. "It seemed like the easi-est way to find you."

Suddenly a sharp male voice from up an aisle was yelling, "Hey! Hey!" We turned to see a clumsy, pear-shaped man coming toward us waving both hands in the air.

"What are you girls doing here? You can't put on some sort of show in our store. We're trying to *sell* things."

I couldn't believe my ears. Hope gave him a dirty look, grabbed my hand, and pulled me toward the checkout stand. "Your mom's going to love that story," she said under her breath.

When she paid for the candy, we looked at each other and burst out laughing. The poor girl counting out change must have thought we were nuts.

On the way out, we stopped at another gumball machine for a plastic egg with junk in it. "Hey, Hope, some day we really ought to learn harmony on some other songs."

"Yeah, but we're so good at that one. Fifty cents," she said, popping a second quarter into the slot. "Your moth-er's right. What a rip-off."

I turned my bubble over and over. For being smaller than a golf ball, it looked like it had a lot of stuff in it.

Hope kept humming as we walked to the car, and when she'd whipped back onto 80, she used her teeth to rip open the cellophane bag of candy orange slices, popped a whole one in her mouth, and made big sucking noises as we headed into the afternoon sun.

I tucked my hands under my thighs and sat stiffly to keep my back off the hot seat. "Too bad Alma wasn't here. She would've liked to hear us, don't you think?"

"Alma, yes." Hope nodded. "You know, Carin, I *never* do karaoke." She giggled like people do when they're nervous. "I don't know what got into me, but then being up there with a microphone—it's what my mom wanted to do her whole life. You know?"

"She did do it for a little while, didn't she, your mom, singing, I mean?"

"I guess so. I mean, she did it at home, in the evenings. I remember her sitting in the living room playing and singing. And then I know she was visiting radio stations and agents in Nashville when she was in the car wreck. I've got to ask Dad again. There must be more."

I couldn't think of any more to say, but Hope didn't seem to want to talk, so we rode in silence for a long time, into the early evening, actually crossing into Utah. When we stopped for gas, we each pulled snacks from the back, and then Hope drove on.

13

I returned to my bracelet, black over red, tie with green, purple under, pull tight. A few more minutes, and I could pull all the threads into a knot.

Done.

Without warning, Hope suddenly pulled off the freeway at Echo and stopped in front of a little motel—the Red Top. We'd passed a few billboards for it, and I thought it looked bigger on the billboard pictures than it did in life.

Hope let her head fall to the steering wheel. "I'm beat. What's our mileage?"

"You've done close to five hundred." I didn't want to say 480, which was more accurate. "It still leaves almost five hundred eighty for tomorrow. Can you handle that?"

She let out a hard breath. "It'll mean no silly shopping or Wal-Mart stops. I've done a lot more in a day, but, man, this heat takes it out of me."

"I'll try to be a more lively rider, too."

"Thanks, Sis. I'll get my alarm so we can get out early."

Hope came out of the office dangling a key from a green plastic rectangle. "Let's go."

The motel was a long white building with six blue doors,

one after the other, all the way to the end, each with a metal number nailed to it. The whole strip of rooms had a single red roof. Hope unlocked our door, number four, and we hauled our stuff inside. The room smelled musty, and the bedspread looked old; it all looked old, especially the brown shaggy rug.

"Mom would want us to keep our shoes on in here."

Hope laughed. "You're right, but we can survive one night. Yes?"

"Sure."

She brought in enough food to call it dinner.

"Hey, we didn't open our plastic bubbles," I reminded her.

"Ah, what treasures await us."

When we went out to the car for our bags, it was nearly nine, and the sun was low in the sky. As I waited for Hope, I played with my shadow, which was so long that it stretched beyond the end of the parking lot clear back to the road. I hopped and swung my arms and stretched all over the place. I felt like a rubber Gumby or like I did in the yard games I'd played with Jenna when we were little. We'd pretend we were Peter Pan, and we'd try to wiggle out of our shadows so that Wendy could stitch them on later.

"I found my nail polish," she said from under the raised hatchback. "Must do *some*thing about these claws now, since my interview's tomorrow."

"Yeah, tomorrow night at this time we'll be at Dad's."

We went inside. Hope didn't look as excited as I thought she would, but she had a lot on her mind.

We dumped the contents of our bubbles on the rickety desk—plastic charms in red, brown, silver, and orange fell out. "We could hang them on our clothesline," I said.

Hope gave me a look. "My guess is that, all totaled, we paid a dollar for about three to four cents' worth of ——," she said.

"Ugh. I guess the other ninety-six cents was for the thrill of turning the handle."

"And for hope. People pay a lot for hope."

She went out to the car and came back with a couple of rumpled shopping bags. "I wanted to have an actual cloth object to take to the interviews—to show her my potential." Hope lifted two huge mounds of fabric from one of the bags. "I bought these two dresses off a ten-dollar rack once. Cool fabric. I knew they'd come in handy some day."

She threw the pink pile at me. "Here, put it on."

I tossed it one way and another to find the top. "It's huge, Hope! I'll look like a puff ball."

"Lots of pink."

I finally had my arms in the armholes and my head in the head hole and shook the thing on. Hope was halfway into something made of green swirls and lots of sparkly bits. Even on tallish me, when the dress slipped onto my shoulders, gobs of fabric landed on the ground. When I moved, the neck slid over one shoulder and I could feel the whole thing dropping off. Hope wasn't doing much better.

"Hold on. I can solve this problem." From the second bag, she drew a pair of long scissors, a box of pins, a plastic sack of ribbons, and a giant glue gun.

"Come stand over here." She waved the glue gun at me, slithered out of her dress, and picked up the scissors.

I obeyed. She dropped to her knees, and began snipping and cutting here and there, lifting strips from the bottom and gluing them higher up. She slowly worked her way toward the top of the dress, gathering fabric together across my back and attaching it with a big hiss from the glue gun. "Don't glue me," I warned.

"Never glued anyone—yet."

She lifted the sides of the skirt and attached them here and there so they looked like flower petals.

"Wow, Hope," I gushed, "this is amazing."

"I think it'll work." She touched my shoulders to turn me round. "Step out now so you can wear the other one."

I slipped into the green one, and she began from the top, slicing the fabric, twisting and gluing strips together, creating something that seemed like a punk-spaceship-flapper dress all in one. Watching her reminded me of Edward Scissorhands, the way she snip, snip, snipped and glued and changed things so quickly into something incredible. When she was finished, we put on the elegant gowns—over our shorts and T-shirts—and curtsied.

"Incredible, Hope. I am totally awed!"

"Thanks. See why I like doing this stuff?"

We cleaned up and she put everything away and finally did her nails. We tried to watch some TV but a layer of thick snow fell in front of every channel. When we fell into bed, we actually *fell* into bed. The mattress center was soft and shaped like a spoon or a crater; Hope and I leaned into each other like puppies.

Toward morning, we kept waking up, pushing our way out of the dip, and grasping our sides of the bed. She got up to go to the bathroom, and after that neither of us could go back to sleep.

She pulled open the curtain on the day. The sky was pale, barely light. "What do you think?" she asked. "The alarm hasn't even gone off, but we've got a long haul."

I nodded and climbed out of the pit. After showering and eating a little, we packed up.

As Hope started the car, she said, "Remind me to check out the bed in any future motels before I pay any money."

"No problem," I said through a yawn.

14

Utah promised to be uneventful. That is, I made a promise to myself that it *would* be uneventful if I had anything to do with it. I'd had enough events for the whole trip.

Since we were driving through the neck of Utah, we had only three counties to go: Summit, Salt Lake, and Tooele. ("It rhymes with Prunella," Hope said, "the uglier of the two ugly stepsisters.") How much trouble could we get into in just three counties?

I believed we'd sail across the state without a single hitch. After all, it was Friday. We had to reach Dad's tonight so Hope could have her job interview. I said a little prayer to help and then pulled out my notebook and atlas to calculate our location.

Distance from Davenport — 1,157 miles
Distance to Reno — 606 miles

"About six hundred miles left, Hope."

"Great. Nine hours at the most. And it's not even seven a.m. We'll be fine."

I put my notebook away and turned to the junky plastic charms from our gumball bubbles. Each one had a hole for a string, so I snipped embroidery floss and looped each one onto the clothesline. "What do you think, Hope?"

"I like the beige elephant," she said. "Too bad it's only a quarter the size of the bright red cowboy boot."

"What about the hats?" We'd found both a top hat and fireman's hat in her bubble.

"Nice motif. Add in the baseball glove and the horse-shoe, and the wardrobe theme is complete."

"Nobody can top us for souvenirs."

To keep us on a steady course, I started watching the landscape in an orderly way, looking at one scene briefly, then moving my head to look at the next one. I felt like a camera recording our trip. *Snap. Snap. Snap.*

The green of Iowa was far behind us now and so were Nebraska and Wyoming. We drove through dusty gray-green hills with sagebrush, low grasses, and patches of wildflowers with blue or yellow blossoms.

If I had taken photos every fifty miles, I could have made a long photo strip of land and color change from Davenport to Reno. I wished I'd thought of it in time. I pulled out my pad and figured how many chunks of fifty miles we'd gone. Eleven hundred and fifty miles would be twenty-three fifty-mile stretches.

I bet Mom would have stitched the photos together for me; she often sewed strange things. Last Halloween she took an old calendar apart and sewed the months into some kind of tunic to make herself into what she announced was "a calendar girl." She thought it was hilarious. I took a photo of her in front of her clocks—how fitting. The "time machine" I called her.

By the time we got to Dad's I could have another twelve photos, which would make thirty-five altogether.

"What are you up to?" Hope said, interrupting my thoughts.

"Math."

"Great. Summer vacation hits, and my little sis spends her free time doing math."

I threw my hands up in the air and smiled at her, then I told her my idea. ". . . and if they were each six inches wide, I'd have a two-hundred-and-sixteen-inch—except for sewing overlap—long stripe of landscape on the wall above my bed and it would wrap around part of the side walls, too. In fact I could get duplicates and Mom could make me one long photo stripe for Iowa and one for Reno."

"Cool," Hope said.

Then, no matter where I was, I thought, I could follow the strip to the other half of my life, and it wouldn't be just a connection like on a phone or from thoughts in your head. The pictures would connect me to this path. I could remember places the first time I'd seen them and maybe remember what the air smelled like and whether or not Hope and I had just had a fight or if we'd done something goofy there or whatever.

The only problem was that to actually create the photo strip, I'd have to make this trip all over again.

"The car looks great by the way," I said. She'd cleaned it out while I showered.

"It needed it. Besides I had a fantasy that maybe we could still get the mannequin inside. A crazy idea."

"It's been okay on top, hasn't it?"

"Yeah. I just don't want it to get ripped off."

I laughed and hoped she didn't hate me for it. "Hope, it's not like a DVD player or something. Not many people would have the eye that you have for such a thing."

"Guess I'm just lucky, aren't I?" She winked at me.

It was still early when we stopped for gas. We were near Wanship.

I went to the bathroom and then back to the car for money. Breakfast in the motel had been a little dry— peanut butter and jelly on rice cakes and some motel water. "Hope," I asked, "want something to eat?"

Hope was hanging onto the gas nozzle. "What are you having?"

I shrugged. "Juice and a donut."

"Get some tall bottles of water for the next leg. And I'll have an ice cream bar."

I wrinkled my nose. "At this hour?"

"Freedom, Carin. It's a great thing. I can eat ice cream any darn time I want."

I must have looked at her funny, because Hope stared at me and laughed. "Or you don't have to eat it ever. Carin? Are you there?"

I pulled out of my daze, watched her pull the nozzle out

of the tank, and screw the cap on. "I'm not ready for ice cream this early."

"Very wise. Take your time with these life-changing decisions." She winked at me. "Get what suits you, but save a few bucks for future gas."

I ate my food and then napped for a while. When I woke up, Hope was swinging us smoothly along the freeway high above Salt Lake City. I looked out over the office buildings and stores and restaurants and wondered if anyone in all of Salt Lake had eaten ice cream for breakfast.

An airplane lifted off the ground to our right, and I couldn't help but wish, just for a second, that I were tucked neatly on board. Oh well.

"You were really sawing some logs there."

"That mattress, I guess."

"Yes. I can hardly wait for a good bed at Dad's."

"I'm sticky again, but that doesn't mean I'm asking for a car wash."

"I know. You can have a real shower at Dad's."

I chewed some gum until it was good and soft, then reached for the candy box and pushed the wad onto the relief map to finish Wyoming and start Utah.

"Can I have a piece?" Hope asked. "Unchewed, if you don't mind."

I handed her one.

"If you want it back for the candy-box map, I'll accommodate," she said with a twinkle in her eyes.

"Thanks but no."

Before long we entered the last county of Utah. It was another one of those giant ones that could hold several Rhode Islands. About forty miles later, the road took a small curve and headed across the Great Salt Lake Desert on a highway that was straight as a needle. Several billboards talked about the Bonneville Salt Flats. "What does that mean, Hope—salt flats?"

"You'll see. Meanwhile, 'Welcome to the Dwight D. Eisenhower Highway,'" Hope read.

"A section of road named after a president?"

"It was his idea, the whole thing."

"What whole thing?"

"The interstate."

It never occurred to me that a road would be somebody's idea.

Hope seemed to be reading my mind. "Everything is somebody's idea first."

Of course she was right, but I'd never had the thought.

My nose was deep in the atlas when Hope bumped me on the arm and pointed to our right. "There it is. Weird enough for you?"

My jaw dropped. Weird was the *only* word for it.

Mountains rose in the distance, but between us and them the flat ground was covered with what looked like a giant white sheet of wedding-cake frosting.

"Salt. Acres and acres of hard salt."

I looked and looked. Not only had I never seen anything like it. I'd never *imagined* anything like it. After a while, the brightness got to me, and I rummaged through my bag for the goofy big dark glasses that Hope had bought us in Wyoming. She laughed.

We drove on a while. The quiet of the road was peaceful, but as the sun rose higher in the sky, creeping up behind us, the inside of the car started growing hot. Hope rubbed her eyes and stretched her shoulders up and down.

"You want to pull over for a while?"

She sighed. "Better not."

"Wish I could drive."

Hope jerked up in her seat and swung sideways. "Yes! Great idea. And I get a two-minute break."

"What? Are you serious?"

"Aren't you?" Hope pulled off the highway, which was level with the salt, and aimed the car northwest—I gave a quick look at my compass. She hopped out. "Let's swap. Come on."

I stepped out of the car slowly.

"Come on," Hope said. "Driving lesson. This is perfect. No roads, no cars, no curbs, nothing to run into or off of."

"Are you sure?"

"I'm so sure, I don't even think it's illegal. It's like driving in your own driveway."

I slipped in behind the driver's seat and pressed my foot on the gas. We flew straight into the whiteness.

"Yippee!" Hope yelled.

I laughed. My stomach was jumping around, but I loved it. I glanced at the speedometer, and it was already up to sixty-five. I lifted my foot and we slowed a little.

"Watch out—we might slide right into the mountains!" she said.

We were miles from the mountains, but it felt like we could skid along forever. I decided to step on the brakes, which I did badly at first. We jerked, which made Hope laugh again. Finally the car stopped, but my heart and stomach were still flying around inside of me.

"Lesson one. You did very well. How do you feel?"

I shook myself a little and shrugged. "Buzzy."

"Buzzy?"

"I don't know. Like I've jumped off a roof or something."

"Great. And you're safe and sound. Now you can turn us around?"

"You're sure relaxed."

"Well, it's pretty impossible to have a wreck here."

Very slowly, I eased the car around and headed back to the highway, much slower. When we got within what would be a few blocks, I stopped. "That's enough." My stomach and my good sense said so.

I got out of the car and waited for Hope.

"You win," she said.

"You thought I'd drive on the highway?"

"Well. . . At least now you've had a lesson. And we're a few hundred feet down from where we were."

"You're wacky sometimes."

"Don't you think big sisters should be wacky some of the time?"

I smiled. I think I expected a big sister to be something else.

While Hope eased us back on the interstate, I glanced at my compass again. The needle wobbled to my right, north, and we were once again headed west.

Even though we'd almost crossed the entire state of Utah—two hundred and some miles—it was not quite noon. Ahead of us was a long, sticky afternoon, with the sun beating on us all the way, but at least we were covering ground.

Signs for Wendover began appearing, and I almost wished I had gone ahead and driven for a while. Hope still had hours at the wheel, all the way across Nevada, before her job interview. She already looked tired. We were both tired.

Hope reached for an ice cube. "Desperate times call for desperate measures." She rubbed it over her face and then held it in her armpit.

"Hope!" I wasn't quite that desperate.

"Ugh! This is very difficult," she squeaked. "But it really helps."

I pulled out the map and opened it, pulled out my notebook again, and figured out where we were.

Distance from Davenport—1,315 miles
Distance to Reno—448 miles

One thing I liked about keeping track of all these numbers was that as soon as I wrote them down, they were history. We were farther along.

Soon we were on a winding road heading into Nevada. *Nevada.*

"We're actually here, Hope."

She gave the steering a wheel a tappity-tap.

The first exit I saw had the number 410 on it—410 miles across the state, which was pretty much where Reno was. Gosh, still a long way to go. Considering how few miles we'd driven some days, it seemed impossible to think we could go 400 more miles today. But we had to.

The next town was Oasis. "Should we stop there?" I asked.

"We'd better. Maybe its name is true and it's the last stop for a long ways."

The Oasis Truck Stop had signs for everything from showers to massages. Hope wanted a bathroom, and we decided to get gas and a quick meal.

When I stepped out of the car, my foot landed on something squishy. "Yuk."

"What?"

I looked down. "Just a hamburger bun, but it felt like a dead bird or something."

"Carin, you have the most gruesome imagination."

"Well, remember old Markham? I grew up with 'gruesome.'"

I locked my door and Hope adjusted the mannequin. Her blanket had slipped.

"What?" Hope asked. "Oh, yes. The cat who liked to bring you a fresh kill now and then."

I popped her. "Fresh yes, sometimes still living." She bopped me back.

"Voices," she said as we left the restroom. I was puzzled for a second before I remembered our old silliness. We walked into the bright and cool restaurant. Several tables ran down the center and there were two rows of booths near the windows. We took a booth. Four women sat down across from us. They wore dresses and looked like they worked in an office.

"Zee cat, zee Markham, vass a—how you say—real pain," Hope said in a French accent as she sent her fingers pointing in random directions.

I waved my hands in the air. We both seemed to wave our hands around a lot when we talked in accents. "But, heee could not help zee fatness. Zee appetite, eet was so big."

"But poor ma*ma*"—Hope motioned wildly—"ven she put less food in heez bowl, zee cat, yes, keeled zee little fresh animals in zee yard, no?"

The waitress came with water and menus. "Soup and salad bar is the special today," she said without looking at us. "Three dollars and ninety-five cents. Or just the soup and bread is two dollars and ninety-five cents."

"Zee soups," I said in my most polite English/French, "vat types are zey?"

The corners of the waitress's mouth rose a little, and she spoke very slowly and a little louder. "Corn chowder and gazpacho—that's cold with tomato juice and lots of vegetables." By the end of her description, she was nodding her head up and down in big movements.

"Zee soup!" Hope said, clapping her hands together.

"And me!" I added.

The waitress motioned to soup pots. "And there's hot bread there, too. You ladies help yourselves."

"Zee hot meal, it is good for us, no?" Hope said.

"Ma*ma* would be zo happy for us."

Hope clicked her tongue against her teeth and said, "Ma*ma* doesn't care beans about zee temperature of zee food eaten by us."

I giggled. We both ladled cold gazpacho into our bowls and cut big slices of hot, fresh bread for ourselves. Next to the bread was a bowl of soft butter, which we gobbed onto the bread. Hot bread is the only way I like butter; it melts all the way in so you don't have to feel that little button of clammy slime in your mouth, which makes me think of an eye from a dead fish.

"Remember how zee cat we called Markham, he brought zee game into zee house? Zee birdies, zee mousies, zee squirrel—"

"—without zee little tail."

"Yuk."

"And zee Mom put zee squirrel in zee freezer because zee garbage pickup was days away."

"Yezzz, but zee Mom, she kept forgetting. It sat in zee chilly air for a month, at least. Next to zee popsicles."

"And she wore zee dark glasses when she vacuumed zee little bits up from zee other dead animals zo she wouldn't know one leetle part from zee other."

Sometimes we stole glances at the table of office

women. They seemed to be enjoying us, which made us enjoy us that much more.

"Zee zoup, eet is wonderful, no?" I asked.

"Zee zoup, eet is grand. But back to zee cat. Recall heez bathroom habits. So rude."

"Zee Papa, he called it, 'Dragging zee keester.'"

"Poor Mama. She wouldn't give zee cat away. 'Who wants a cat zat wipes himself on zee furniture,' she would zay."

Hope looked up at me from her soup. "And would you like zees cat now? On our leetle trip? Dragging zee keester all over zee leetle car?"

I laughed. "No. No zank you very much."

15

Outside again, we did a few quick jumping jacks and hit the road.

"Hey, Hope. You know all these strangers we keep bumping into? A few icks, but then Alma in Nebraska? Chuck? The people at the reunion. How do you know if they're safe or not?"

"I don't."

These words were not what I expected. I wanted to hear some big-sister wisdom.

"My thinking is this," she said as she pulled back onto the Interstate. "Most people in the world are a lot like everybody else—friendly and helpful. There are wackos, but they don't wear signs, so I'm nice to people and give them a chance to be nice back. That's what usually happens."

I was silent a minute, thinking about the word *usually* and recalling that even Hope had described herself as a wacky sister. "But—"

"I do what feels right, and hope it works out. *Hope*—get it? It's in my blood."

I wondered if I'd ever be as casual as Hope about life.

Probably not. I reached for my atlas and notebook—my ways of keeping the world in order.

We had fifty miles to Elko, which was about a quarter of the way across Nevada.

"Homestretch," I said.

"Almost," Hope said, looking a little anxious.

"And we gained an hour when we crossed from mountain daylight time to Pacific on the Nevada border."

"Excellent," said Hope. "I'd forgotten about that."

It was about one o'clock when we reached Elko. We stopped at a Holiday Inn and used their big, clean bathroom. On the way back through the lobby, I spotted a row of slot machines. "Hope, look." I pulled on her shirt and made her stop. "Do you have some change?"

She gave me a funny look and stuffed her fist into her shorts. When she opened her hand, it had three quarters in it.

"Do it!" I shoved my hand into my pocket and touched the wishbone for good luck.

She popped the coin into the slot and hit the button. Lights flashed on and off as though something wonderful was about to happen, but a lemon, a strawberry, and an orange came up in a row, and that was the end of the show.

"Try it once more," I urged.

She pushed one more quarter through the slot. I was surprised she wasn't more into it. The thrill seemed like something she'd like.

Her push of the button produced another anxious hype of sound and light. Nothing else.

"One more?" I asked reluctantly.

She held up the last quarter by its thin edge and turned it one way and the other. Into the slot went the coin, on went the lights and buzzers, and then—yippee—the sound of coins clinking into the cup by our knees. She reached down and scooped them up. "Let's go," she said before I could say anything.

A gruff voice said, "Hey, hey!" It was a man at the desk giving us a dirty look. "You kids get away from there."

I looked up. A sign above my head stated in clear terms that people my age weren't allowed to operate the machines or be in the area, and Hope wasn't looking particularly adult herself.

"How much did you get?" I asked as soon as we were outside.

"Six of them. A dollar and a half. Enough gambling. Boy, Carin. You could really get sucked in."

"The machine is cool," I said defensively.

"Yeah, but it's made to win. Just like those gumball machines."

"I know, I know." I felt a little stupid.

We drove along the frontage road until we reached a gas station. Hope pulled in but didn't park by a pump.

"What's wrong?"

"We've got to count up resources here. Things are tight."

My mouth went dry. Now that we were actually in Nevada, weren't we too close for anything to go wrong?

"Here's the story." Hope opened her wallet. Two dollar

143

bills gaped open like the last two pitiful petals on a flower. She looked at me.

"That's it?!" I exploded.

"And the miracle money we just made in the slot machines. I thought one of these bills was a five until I paid for our lunch. The gas tank is about empty, we're down to whatever's in back, foodwise, and we've got about"—she looked thoughtful for a minute—"three hundred and some miles to go."

"How could you let that happen!? You had the three hundred dollars. It's your job interview! Where did it go?"

She sat silent, and I felt awful—mad at her and scared and mad at myself. I thought about dozens of things all at once—the waffle iron, ice cream bars, bags of ice, extra pieces of pie, Cokes, snacks, our goofy big glasses, money leaving us for all kinds of things. I resented her and this road trip all over again, and I nursed my poor-pitiful-me feelings like a fresh scrape, though I was determined to keep them to myself. I pulled my backpack onto my lap, dug around, and dumped my coin purse into my lap. A wadded bill fell out and some change.

"I don't suppose there's any chance that bill is a five," Hope said quietly.

I unwound it into full size and held it up tightly. "Number ones" glared at us from all four corners, and a big fat ONE occupied the middle. I counted the rest of the change. "And forty-three cents. I'm sorry I yelled. We're in this together. It's my fault, too."

"Carin, your fault? I don't think so. If there's blame

144

to be taken here, it's me who gets it. But thanks."

Neither of us said anything for a while. I felt surprise at her words. I couldn't remember Hope ever taking blame for things. My own words surprised me, too. But I'd said them, and it was true. I should have paid more attention to my just-in-case funds. A crisis is exactly what it's for. After the car broke down in Hershey, I thought our worries were over.

Hope bit her bottom lip and then took a big deep breath. "So we've got four dollars and ninety-three cents. It'll get us about three or so gallons of gas and forget any food. Who knows how accurate the gas gauge is—especially on the empty side. We might be in better shape than we think, but whatever—it's not enough to get us to Reno."

We sat back for a minute. I couldn't believe Hope didn't have any credit cards, but I knew it was true. She'd *had* them at some point, but they'd been trouble.

"Any bright ideas yet?" she asked.

"Nope. You?"

"Nope."

We sat for a few more minutes.

"You know, Hope"—I was trying to think more openly, the way Hope did—"maybe we can find someone who'll do a favor for us. Remember when we were little and we'd go to fast-food places, and you'd be short a bit and con people out of money?"

"Con—I wasn't conning them. I just asked them. Sometimes we'd order a little more than I had change for."

"Yeah, right."

"Sometimes I did it to cute boys, just for fun."

I laughed in spite of my sorry mood.

"That's possible."

Hope nodded and eased the car toward the pumps and squeezed the handle until four dollars and ninety, ninety-one, ninety-two, then ninety-three cents worth of gas had trickled into the tank. She scooped up all of our money and went to the cashier.

"They don't have any work for us," she said as she slid into her seat, "but I can fill our old water bottles."

"Rice cakes and water," I said. "I guess a lot of people do with less."

"Well, not for long."

"We only have to last another four or five hours."

As Hope steered back toward the interstate, she said, "We'll just pull into town after town until we find some help or run out of gas. Dad *could* wire us something if push comes to shove, but I'd rather not hassle it."

"Or Mom," I reminded her.

"Yeah. I can't believe we won't find some helpful soul."

Hope had bought 3.6 gallons of gas, and we'd been getting 28 to 32 miles to the gallon. I took out my pen and paper and figured out the numbers.

"We've just purchased 115.2 miles." I opened the atlas again and put the best face on my report. "That puts us nearly to Winnemucca. Gosh, Hope, that's only 150 miles from Dad."

"We'll make this work, Carin. Remember, the tank

wasn't totally drained. Don't worry." She glanced at the clock. "And it's not even two? We're great for time."

"But if we drive off 80 into every little town, we'll use up gas that way, too."

"Well, we won't go to ones if they don't look good from the highway. What's big before Winnemucca?"

I looked at the map. "Battle Mountain. Population 3,542." Other towns were so small they had no population listing at all. I didn't tell Hope. She had enough to worry about.

We drove on for a while. I wanted to pretend that if we stayed in the car and drove carefully, our gas would get us to Reno. It was like a little-kid wish, and I knew it wouldn't work, but I wanted it badly.

"Another thing we could do," Hope said with a faraway look in her eye as she fingered the jade necklace from her mother, "is find a secondhand shop in Winnemucca and hock Mildred the mannequin. Of course, since I paid only eight dollars for it, and it's only half a mannequin and takes up a lot of space, I might be lucky to get two dollars for it. If they'd buy it at all."

"Two dollars is two dollars."

"True."

I'd thought about selling Mildred, too, but I'd grown to like her on top of the car. She was like a lookout for us. "Well, what about the waffle iron? It's not so rare."

"Another buck or two," Hope said, staring straight ahead. "We'll see."

We drove on. The needle measuring gas was below the

quarter mark, and I found myself holding my breath again and again, as if that could make a difference.

Signs for Battle Mountain began to appear.

"Heck, Carin, let's go straight for Winnemucca. Things are either going to work out there for us or not. If not, we'll call a parent and that will be that."

I nodded and suddenly felt a whole lot better. We had a plan, a definite plan. And we'd be staying on 80 until Winnemucca. Things would work out. Some clouds rolled down on us from the north. We both leaned forward to give our backs relief from the wet, sticky seats.

"Man, that feels good."

Since the ice was gone, along with any money to buy new ice, the sudden cloud cover was a small miracle.

Hope smiled. She looked tired but calm, which helped me feel better. I leaned back in my seat and, without meaning to, drifted off to sleep.

When I woke up, we were right on top of an exit for Winnemucca. "Gosh, I'm sorry I slept so long." I leaned over to look at the gas gauge. The needle was leaning hard toward *E.*

"Not a problem. My anxiety level has done a good job of keeping me on high alert." She pulled the car to the right and joined the Winnemuccans who were doing their Friday errands. I wondered if any of them were at this moment anxious about their nearly empty gas tanks.

"Nerve-wracking, isn't it." Hope drove up one street and down another and suddenly pulled into a parking lot. "I have an idea." She jumped out of the car and bolted around the corner of an auto-parts store. In minutes, she was back, clutching a ten-dollar bill. "We're home free!"

"Where did that come from?"

She wiggled her head back and forth in a teasing way. "A little bird gave it to me."

She whipped the car around and drove to a gas station we'd passed—both of us looking at it enviously—a short time earlier. In a minute, she was back in the car, plopping a bag of ice between us. "I put eight dollars in the tank. We should be golden for getting to Dad's."

"How many gallons?"

"Five. It's more expensive here."

"Close, huh?" I said.

"Yes, but it'll work. And we've got a little cash left."

She patted me on the knee and we headed out the way we had come. I wondered where she'd gotten the money.

We pulled past the auto-parts store. Next to it was a glass repair shop and a boarded-up brick building. Then there was a smaller store with a neon sign inside flashing ARNIE'S PAWNSHOP. I looked at the rope above our heads. Mildred was still on top of the car. I looked around the car frantically, like I had at the St. Vincent's store. It was harder to notice something—you didn't know what—that was gone than it was to find something—you didn't know what—that was already there. What was missing? Hope squirmed, and her fingers flew to her neck, like they did fifty times a day to fidget with her necklace. But she dropped her hand right away. It was gone! "HOPE! NO! Your mom's necklace?! You pawned it!?"

She wouldn't even look at me. "I had to do something," she yelled.

"But that?" I yelled back.

"It'll be fine."

"But Hope—"

"Done! I had to do it. I'm responsible here."

"Responsible? Selling that?! We should have called the parents."

Hope pounded her fist on the steering wheel.

"Carin, calm down. It's responsible because it's short-term. Pawnshops don't sell things for thirty days. I'll send him the money."

"Hope," I yelled.

"Look, Carin." She twisted sideways to look at me. "I'm the one who has to get to Reno tonight. I'm sure my mom would totally approve. Who knows what family heirlooms she gave up to afford her trip to Nashville?"

I bit my lip. "Everything is so messed up. This is a crazy trip, Hope! I never know what's going to happen."

"Well, that's right! Every day, anywhere, you never know what will happen."

"Ooof!" I wanted to shout at her about the money and about being an adult and about—I didn't know what. Why couldn't she plan better?

"Things'll be okay. We've got gas. We'll get there in time for my interview. You'll get to Dad's. It'll all work out." She patted my leg again. "Let's take it easy."

I leaned back and took a deep breath. Relieved to be rescued. Mad that we needed it.

We turned onto the entrance lane for 80 and rode without talking for a while.

"Okay, Carin, we're on the homestretch." Hope touched my arm. "You know those pneumatic tubes they use at the drive-through banking windows? That's us. We aren't stopping until we reach Dad's house. I won't even smile at hitchhikers or kids in cars or passing truck drivers. And you—no more gasping over single shoes or piles of hay you think might be some dead animal. Nothing else is going to go wrong. And needless to say, we won't need to come up with any more creative ways to raise money."

"What if I have to pee?"

"We'll stop for peeing."

I took a deep breath to clear my head.

"Well, our adrenaline got quite a shot, didn't it?" She smiled.

I laughed with her. We were going to make it. Maybe I hadn't given Hope enough credit. She'd messed everything up, but then she'd figured out a way to solve it. Maybe that was what it meant to be an adult.

We drove down our last long stretch of Interstate 80 with our minds glued on Reno. We both might have been picturing Dad's house and his big grin. We'd tell him our harrowing tales, and he'd lean back, all relaxed, and just laugh. *Well, you made it just fine, didn't you?* I could imagine him saying. *You girls can handle things all by yourself.* And I'd be thinking, *Oh, Dad, if you only knew.*

I think we rode for an hour in silence. Sometimes Hope rapped her fingers on the steering wheel like she was tapping out a song, and a few times I saw her put her hand to her throat, forgetting her necklace was gone. Knowing there was gas in the tank gave me—no, both of us—a sense of peace, I thought. Hope was yawning more and more, though. I was tired, too, even with my naps. Gosh, we'd started the day in eastern Utah before a single rosy finger of dawn showed in the sky.

"Well, Carin, you haven't talked about your own plans lately. You know, when you're grown. Math teacher, wasn't it?"

"Right. We need to talk to help you stay alert, don't we."

"Caffeine substitute—okay. But I want to know, too."

"Okay." It made me feel good actually that she'd asked. "I'm not so sure about teaching. I like numbers a lot, though. They're tidy—everything's a zero through nine in some grouping or other—and they mean definite things."

She glanced at me. "Numbers are good. Banking, construction, engineering, baking. Maybe you could invent an umbrella for cars so we could drive in the shade on trips like this."

I smiled. "Yeah. Something like that."

"No! I know. Mapmaking. You have to be a mapmaker."

"I might like that."

"I understand that number thing," Hope added. "That's what I do, too."

I jerked my head around. "What?"

"Measuring. You know? I have to make things fit together. A half inch off can be a disaster."

"Yeah," I said somewhat numbly. I sat calmly in my seat,

but my mind was racing around the car. I hadn't thought of Hope as being a person who was careful about details. "I have to tell you that I never expected to hear you say something like 'A half inch off could be a disaster.'"

She laughed and swung her elbow at me. "You'd be surprised."

I took my Whitman's Sampler box out and opened some more gum to chew. "Here." I handed a piece to Hope. "Maybe it'll help you stay awake."

She popped it into her mouth. "Thanks. Do you want me to contribute it to your project there?"

I chuckled. "No, for the second or third time. I'm impressed that you're so generous with your ABC gum—"

"ABC?"

"Already Been Chewed. You can keep it for yourself, thanks. My own piece will finish the relief map."

"And what a relief *that*'ll be."

We smiled.

I chewed for a while and then added the last gob to finish Utah and Nevada. I pressed the black thread that was my Interstate 80 firmly into place. At the spot that was Reno, I stuck in half a toothpick with four colors of embroidery thread dangling like a pitiful little flag. It was sad that maps, no matter what kind, were so different from what was real. I thought of the photographs at home in my dresser drawer and how they could remind me of the whole day, but they also captured just the tiniest moment. Maps were like that, too, with their circles for cities and nothing but a wiggling line for a river. And relief maps with little lumps pretending to be mountain ranges. None of these things was much like the real thing at all, but I still liked them.

Hope tried to stifle a yawn.

"Let's sing 'The Star-Spangled Banner,'" I suggested.

We did, and she said it was good for her oxygen intake.

A Kraft truck passed us and on the side was a big advertisement for Philadelphia Cream Cheese. "Hope, what if that semi contains nothing but cream cheese. How many packages would it be, do you think?

"You're the mathematician."

I was too hot to tackle such a big problem. All I could think about was how cool it must be inside that truck.

We passed signs for the Rye Patch State Recreation Area and for a few towns. I took out the map. The counties of Humboldt, Lander, Eureka, and Elko were history, and we were deep into Pershing. "Hope," I said in an announcement voice. "We have only Churchill and Storey counties left, and we're done. Done!"

"I suppose we're going to get a final count on the counties?"

"Of course. Eventually."

"Why not . . ." She yawned again.

I grinned and checked my compass. We were headed southwest, as we should have been. Signs for Sparks and Reno started showing up frequently: 78 miles, 72, 63, 54, 47. I pulled out my notebook to make the numbers official. We were so close, I felt butterflies in my stomach.

Distance from Davenport — 1,716 miles
Distance to Reno — 47 miles

I looked at Hope again. She looked like she was sleeping with her eyes open; they were aimed straight ahead so stiffly that they looked like plastic.

I was trying not to think about my bladder, but it would not be ignored. "I'm sorry to say it, Hope, but I need a bathroom."

"No problem." The car suddenly drifted over on the bumps that are supposed to keep you from falling asleep, and Hope jumped. The next exit was only a few miles away.

How easy this stop was compared to the one in Nebraska, where I had to run into the weeds.

"You look pretty tired," I said.

"I am. It'll be good to walk around for a few minutes."

When we pulled off the interstate, we had to go down a frontage road a while to reach a gas station. She pulled two quarters out of her pocket. "Here. Buy some sunflower seeds or something, since you're using their restroom."

Hope's head was on the steering wheel when I got back. "How much is left?" she asked without raising it an inch.

"Not even fifty miles. Less than an hour."

She picked up her head and looked at the car's clock. "And it's only half past six? Isn't that great. We could practically walk."

"What time do you want to get to Dad's?" I asked.

"Well, enough to clean up for the interview. Between nine and ten. I should aim for nine, like a good employee." She smiled and leaned her head back.

"Hope, you're so tired that you almost sound drunk."

She made a small smile. "I know." She spoke slowly. "Since we're in such good shape, let me stretch out for ten minutes, okay? Or twenty. I feel dizzy. I don't want to get us in a wreck."

"That's a great idea. We're fine for time—even with a shower."

She moved the car to a spot under a big tree by a picnic table.

When she parked, I opened my door. "Sit on my side so you can stretch out more."

She obeyed without a word.

I gave her shoulders a massage when she sat down.

"Aaah, you are the greatest. Now if I fall asleep, you wake me. Understood?"

I nodded.

16

Hope was snoring so hard I was sure she'd wake herself up. If Alma's cat had been around, Hope would have been a prime target. It was scary that she could actually sleep through all the racket.

I was tired, too, but not like Hope. I sat at the nearby picnic table and picked at the flaking paint. A guy was throwing a Frisbee over and over to his dog. He threw me a look a couple of times, so I shifted my position, but remembering what Hope had said about strangers, I thought he was probably just some decent guy throwing a Frisbee to his dog.

I stared into space for a while, listening to Hope snore. Not many minutes passed before I began to feel impatient. We were stopped, making no gains at all. Reno was stuck in the ground where it was, we were sitting by a gas station, still nearly fifty miles away, I thought. Something was wrong about this arrangement, and I began to feel the seconds pass like gongs on Cinderella's clock.

The guy and his dog got back into a car. He gave me a little wave as they drove away. There he was, going on his way, and as I watched his car disappear around a bend, I knew what I had to do.

I went back to the car where Hope was totally sacked out. I felt an unexpected surge of tenderness for her and knew I was making the right decision. I eased the car door shut, which didn't do a thing to interrupt her sleep, and slipped into the driver's side. My driving lesson on the salt flats was fresh in my mind. I knew I could drive a little while, and every mile would help. When I turned the key, a storm of butterflies burst open in my stomach. Too bad. I had a job to do.

Easing the car into reverse, I backed out of the space. So far, so good. The parking area was empty, and there was plenty of room for someone like me to get organized. Hope snorted but kept on sleeping.

We started going forward, and I was a little jerky with the steering wheel, because I was trying to think about pushing the gas pedal evenly and not too hard. *So much to concentrate on.*

The frontage road was fairly empty, and when I looked to my left, I could see that not far away cars on the interstate were going much faster. I wasn't ready for that much speed, but I knew frontage roads always led to another interstate entrance, so that's where I'd drive. The sun was getting close to the horizon, and when I followed the road straight west the hot rays hit me bang in the eyes.

"I'll just drive five or ten minutes, and then I'll wake her," I said to myself.

Up ahead, a flashing red light dangled over the intersection. There was a stop sign, too, in case drivers didn't get the message. A few cars were in line, waiting their turn. I pressed on the brake a little early and the car bucked as it moved to the line, but Hope slept on.

When it was my turn to go, I couldn't make my foot press hard enough on the gas. I didn't want to skid across the intersection, because everyone would know I wasn't a real driver, and the cops would be on me in a minute. Another driver kept waving at me, but finally she just threw her hand up in the air and pulled through the inter-section. The guy behind me honked, which frazzled me. I slammed on the gas and lurched forward. Hope started making some new noises, and I thought, *OK, that's enough,* but she shifted and kept on sleeping. My choice was to drive under the interstate or veer a little right. The road to the right made sense, and I took it.

When I remembered to look in the rearview mirror, I saw that the guy behind me was gone; he must have turned. What a relief, but my stomach was still somewhere in space and I was sweating way more than anyone would from the heat.

The frontage road twisted a bit one way and the other. The road was narrow, nothing like driving on the salt flats. I had a few cars behind me, which made me wonder if I was going fast enough. The speedometer said twenty-five, which felt plenty fast, but maybe it wasn't. Ahead, there was a fork in the road. The right one had a guardrail and looked freshly paved. I stayed on it and soon passed a sign that said WADSWORTH, followed by a restaurant, gas station, library, floral shop, and a few things I didn't have time to pay attention to.

Pretty soon, I was passing houses; in one yard some kids were doing cartwheels and jumping jacks, in another they were hopping through a sprinkler. Yards grew bigger, houses fewer, and I expected the interstate entrance to show up soon. When it did, I'd wake Hope. I was ready to be a passenger again.

At least no more cars followed me. I let out a big breath and drove on. Hope was going to be so happy that she had gotten a nap and that we were closer to Reno.

The road twisted and turned and led up and down little foothills, so the driving felt trickier all the time. On both sides of the road, the desert was pebbled with sagebrush, tumbleweeds, and cactus—the low ones that look like a serving platter filled with thick, green, spike-covered leaves. I fell on one my first summer in Nevada.

The road went on and on, and my stomach began to have a hollow space that kept growing larger. I wondered if I should wake Hope. A Jeep jammed with boys suddenly drove up behind me, slowed a little, and whipped around me. One of them gave a friendly wave that I watched through the feathers of dust raised by their tires.

Dust. The pavement had become dusty. That didn't seem like a good sign for a road on its way to the interstate.

Time to turn around. I started looking frantically for any space flat enough for turning. I needed more room than the average person, the average *driver*, I thought. I came up a rise, and ahead were folds of more foothills and beyond, the distant Sierras. No interstate. No sign of life at all. The hole in my stomach stretched another few inches.

Then the car hiccuped.

Hope lifted her head and shook it.

The car burped, and she sat up, awake. "What!"

I pushed on the gas, but we were slowing. I pushed it harder, all the way to the floor, but the speedometer needle slid to fifteen, to ten, and then down to zero as I pulled the car over to the side.

"Carin! What?!" she said again.

"Hope, I— Something's wrong with the car." I wanted to throw up.

I looked at the gas gauge. The dial showed the red hand across the *E*.

"Where are we? What's going on?"

Hope sat up and looked outside at the emptiness. She looked at me questioningly, and she tilted her head over to look at the gauge. She dropped back onto her seat. "Out of gas?!" Her forehead pinched up between her eyebrows, almost like she was asking herself instead of me.

"I wanted to help."

"After all this!? We're out of gas?" Her voice was caught somewhere between a sob and a shout.

She slapped her cheeks to wake herself up. "Help!" She whipped her head around one way and then the other. "Help? You were supposed to wake me up. What happened? Look where we are, Carin! Look!" she shouted.

I didn't have to look, I knew exactly what was outside. Instead, I looked at the clock on the dashboard. I couldn't believe it. I'd been driving for almost half an hour. It was half past seven.

"How did this happen? What are you doing driving?" She jumped out of the car. "Where *are* we?" she yelled into the sky.

"I'm sorry."

"Last I knew I was taking a nap at a gas station." She looked around again. "This looks like the Land of Nowhere."

Tears filled up around my eyes, but I stared hard at the steering wheel so I wouldn't cry.

"Carin, talk to me!"

Out of gas *and* lost. How had I messed up so completely?

"What time is it, anyway?"

I was afraid to say it out loud. I knew it would be more true then. "A little past seven-thirty."

Hope slapped her forehead. "My interview!"

I started crying. "I've screwed up everything."

She scowled. "Yes, you have! About everything's wrong that could possibly go wrong."

"What'll we do?" I cried.

"I don't know," she said and stomped down the road.

She was leaving me!

"Where are you going?!" I bawled and jumped out of the car.

Her voice was full of sharp anger. "I want to find out if I can see *anything* from here."

I sank against the hot car. How could I have been so, so dumb?

It took her several minutes to reach the next crest. I held my breath, hoping she would see civilization. She stood with her hands on her hips, looking into the distance, one way and the other. Then she hopped around and threw her arms every which way and let out a terrible, awful, long scream. I knew she'd only seen more foothills, more sand, more sagebrush.

When she turned and started back, disappointment showed in her every step.

I buried my face in my hands, feeling the seconds tick away. I *hated* being lost. It was the worst feeling in the world.

A few minutes later, Hope pulled one hand off my face. "Okay, listen up. I know you wanted to help. We all do stupid things sometimes."

Not me, I thought, except it wasn't true any longer. I'd just done a whole string of them. "But this one was *so* stupid," I said.

"Look, you did something you had no business doing. Driving?! But—" She interrupted herself. "Is there any Kleenex left from your mom? You're seriously dripping."

I reached for my backpack and dug them out.

"But here's the thing," she went on.

I wiped my face.

"This trip is my responsibility. Didn't we cover this ground before? It's *me* on the crazy schedule. *I'm* the one who wants to get to Reno tonight. It was nuts—I'm the big sister here."

I blew my nose.

She began again. "It was nuts for me not to plan better for daily mileage. I've done more than my share of stupid things. You know that as well as anyone. If I lose this job— well, I can't be mad at you about it."

A new wave of tears covered my eyes. I felt like such a dope. "But we were so close to making it, Hope! Everything was going so perfectly!"

Hope shrugged. "Perfect might be a stretch."

"How can you not be screaming mad at me?" I shrieked.

"So you didn't hear me?" She gave me a hug and nodded in the direction of the hill she'd climbed. "Look, we're here. There's no way to undo anything. Now what we have to do is save ourselves."

"You're being so nice, Hope."

"Getting mad isn't going to get us out of here. Would you feel better if I yell some more?"

I laughed a little. "Maybe."

"Let me be nice once in a while, okay?"

I wiped my nose some more. "Oh, Hope. I've been so unfair."

"What? Driving without a license? Yes."

"No. When you started walking away, I thought you were leaving me."

Hope's mouth dropped open. "Leave you! Here?"

"See? I keep expecting you to do something that makes me mad or hurts my feelings. Or scares me. I mean, it's not like you do it all the time, but—"

"Look, Carin, I know I did that stuff in the past, when I

was younger. But, I don't *want* to hurt you. Please stop expecting it. What can I say?"

"It's me. I'm sorry. I let myself expect it."

"Let it go, Carin. It'll eat you up. Both of us."

I knew she was right. Why did I keep hauling around bad stuff like it was so valuable. I blew out a huge breath, as if I could blast all of it out in one giant balloon of air. I wished I could.

"Carin, some time in the future—it won't be on purpose, I promise—I'm sure I *will* do things that disappoint you or hurt you."

We looked at each other for a moment.

"We're family after all!" she said. We froze for a second and then we hugged and laughed. Or maybe cried. Who knew which, who cared.

Hope sniffed. "I guess I could use a Kleenex, too," she said. "So tell me the details. How *did* we end up in never-never land? Then we have to plan a strategy for getting out of it."

17

"**I was** trying to help. I thought I could drive just a short way . . . ," I began. By the time I finished my story, I was sniffling again.

Hope tossed the Kleenex pack to me. "These are about gone. Good thing, too. We've got to stop dehydrating ourselves." She leaned over and patted my arm. "What a day, my dear sister, what a day."

I pulled out the last tissue. A folded piece of lined paper came with it. "What's this?"

Shadows suddenly appeared on the ground around us. Hope pointed up. "Great. Look, Carin. Buzzards." We laughed and she yelled into the sky, "I hope this is some kind of joke."

I unwound the paper and saw Mom's writing. "Listen to this, Hope. 'If you're reading this note, you must be sick, dirty, or crying. For whatever reason, here's something that might help.'" I kept unfolding, and out fell a twenty-dollar bill.

I waved it in the air. Hope's jaw dropped and her eyes opened as big as quarters. She kept saying, "Oh!" over and over, until she looked squarely at me. "If anything else happens today, I'm just—I don't know . . ." She gave out a big sigh, but it sounded happy. "Now we're stranded, but we're rich. Ironic, isn't it?"

"Hope, you look—you look almost happy. What about the job interview?"

"Well, here I am in costume land. If this one doesn't work, there'll be others. What matters at the moment is getting the two of us rescued."

I stood back from the car and looked at the sign in the window. WEST WITH HOPELESS. I felt bad. "Hope? I'm sorry about the sign. I should change it back to WESTWARD HO!"

"No way. Some day when we have kids and we tell them about what we did before they were born, we'll both have the WEST WITH HOPELESS trip."

"Today I think it should be WEST WITH HELPLESS."

"That'd be my version, Sis." She laughed and bopped me on the arm.

I bopped her back. "Hey, Sis yourself."

"All right!"

"Here, you keep charge of this." I tucked the bill in her pocket.

A vulture squawked above us. Hope tipped her head back and used her hand as a visor to shelter her eyes against the sun. "If we could call that old buzzard down here and tie this bill around his neck with directions to where we are . . . if we only knew where we were." She suddenly turned to me. "Map Girl, ideas?"

"I know we were in Wadsworth. And another road that I didn't take led to Sutcliffe and Nixon." I looked at my compass. "We're facing straight west. We should be going southwest."

"Hmmm."

"Hope, I'm sorry. Our map doesn't even have this road on it. I didn't know there were roads that weren't on the map. I wouldn't have been so sure of myself."

Hope smiled. "See? The mapmakers need you."

"Hey, I didn't tell you—a carload of kids passed us before you woke up, so this road leads somewhere."

"Good news! We're not in the middle of Nowhere, we're in the middle of Somewhere. The question is if we should go backward or forward, or if we should just stay put."

We sat back down in the car to get out of the sun.

Miracle, miracle, I thought. I felt my shorts pocket for the wishbone, to see if there was any help there. "Is there anything we could lay down for planes to see?"

"There's no question the parents will call out the National Guard when we don't show up, so we've got to get cracking with something."

We sat in silence another minute. Some rumble in the distance caught our attention at the same moment.

"A helicopter!" Hope shouted, and we hopped out of the car and jumped up and down, shouting and waving. It drifted toward us and then away.

"Shoot!"

"Pilots could hardly see us anyway," Hope said. "The car probably looks like a big stone with—"

"—with half a woman on top? Maybe Mildred will be useful here. You and I—we look like desert rocks."

We both wore khaki shorts and white T-shirts. "Nothing about us is bright. We should have packed something Day-Glo orange."

"Carin, you're brilliant! Those dresses."

"*Those* dresses?"

In the next few seconds, Hope had the pink and green dresses out of the bag, and we pulled them over our clothes.

"Now we are desert flowers, dancing desert flowers, visible from the sky. We must be investigated. Besides, it's driving me nuts to wait around. I've got to *do* something."

"But, Hope, you and I sing, we don't dance."

"We dance now. When was the last time you sat in an auditorium—"

"December. *The Nutcracker Suite.*"

"*The Nutcracker!* Perfect."

"What?"

"The 'Dance of the Sugarplum Fairies.'"

"Of course! How obvious. Except, I don't *know* the 'Dance of the Sugarplum Fairies.' Do you?"

Hope opened her hands and wiggled her eyebrows. "Us? Are you kidding? I'll start with the ti ti ti's and you can take over the dum, dum, dum's. It'll be grand. Follow me!"

Ti ti ti ti ti-ti ti-ti-ti ti-ti-ti ti-ti-ti ti ti ti ti ti.

Hope pointed at me and I sang.

Dee-dle dee-dle dum.

And on we went, Hope leading as we pranced to the rise in the road and began winding into spirals and swooping circles, our colorful, silky dresses swishing like soft wings behind us. "Be Isadora Duncan!" she shouted at a break in her line.

"Who's she?" I called back when I had a chance.

"First modern dancer!" Hope yelled as she sang or screamed her notes. "Lots of arm waving, lots of turns!"

"I can do that!" I shouted. But I could shout better than I could dance.

"First dancer to dance barefoot!"

"Really!?"

"Big scandal!"

Dee-dle dee-dle dum.

"Long ago!" I called back.

"Yes! Not our forevers!" shouted Hope.

18

We twirled and twisted in our swishy dresses and sang at the top of our lungs to the setting sun. Near the edge of the Earth where the sun was lounging, two long gauzy strips of fierce pink appeared taped to the sky. I wanted to think they were healing the damage of the day, comforting all, and I danced harder and sang louder to loosen all the old thoughts I wanted to cast away. *Out, out stupid angers, away, away useless whining!* I felt freer and freer, even though we were stuck in the desert.

Suddenly a noise louder than our singing crashed around us, and a motorcycle came over the next hill, heading right at us. We stood in the road and waved our arms. The cyclist pulled up and shut down his engine. He pulled off his helmet and sat there, looking at us.

I guess both Hope and I were so shocked that neither of us said anything for a minute.

"Need some help?" he said finally. He had light brown hair pulled into a ponytail and a mustache as thick as a brush.

"Yes, actually," Hope said in a careful tone.

I, on the other hand, was practically ready to kiss the guy's feet.

"I ran out of gas," Hope said. "Can you believe it?"

Hope! It was *me* who ran out of gas.

The fellow nodded and looked up and down at our dresses.

Hope followed his eyes. "We thought we might attract the attention of any search planes or helicopters flying over."

"Just the thing."

He crossed his arms and leaned back as if he were sitting on a porch somewhere waiting for the sun to go down, which it almost had.

"Name's Michael," he said.

"Can you help us?" I said bluntly. I couldn't stand this polite chitchat that was getting us nowhere. We already *were* nowhere, and I wanted to be *some*where.

Michael looked at his watch. "I'm headed into Reno for a concert."

"You mean this road actually goes into Reno?" I held my breath.

"Yeah, we natives use it. Not too much traffic."

"Yes!" I couldn't contain myself, even if it was dumb luck.

"We noticed," Hope said, "about not too much traffic."

"There's a station up there a few miles," he said, nodding in the direction the car was facing. "I could take one of you."

Hope and I looked at each other. My mood took a nose-dive. She'd have to be the one to go. I'd have to be the one to stay. Alone. Out here.

Michael's words interrupted the thoughts screaming back and forth between us. "You don't see that sort of stuff out here very often." He motioned toward our dresses. "What I'm worried about is that, uh, that cloth getting caught in my wheel."

"Right, right. Just a sec," Hope said, and disappeared around the car. In a flash, she was back in her shorts and shirt again.

"That's better," he said.

"My name's Hope, by the way, and this is Carin."

We all shook hands. I could feel my heart pounding with the excitement of being saved or maybe it was the fear of being abandoned in the darkening desert.

"Joe's station is a ways up. I'll take you there. They oughta be able to bring you back eventually." Michael's mustache slid up a bit on his face. Maybe he smiled.

Eventually. What did that mean?

"Are we very far from Reno?" Hope asked.

Michael tilted his head one way and then the other. "Twenty minutes from downtown, I suppose. That's where I'm headed. Willie Nelson's in town. Can you beat that? The old codger. I wouldn't miss him."

Willie Nelson. Was it only three days ago that I looked at that used tape in Iowa City? *On the Road Again.* Now I wish I'd bought it, except if I had, our money problems would have started $2.99 earlier. I wondered if Willie'd ever had a road trip as odd as ours.

He nodded to Hope. "Ready?"

She looked at me and climbed on behind him. I bit my lip.

Michael stomped on the lever that started the motorcycle and put his helmet back on.

Hope waved me over. I bent down and she pulled my ear close to her mouth. "Get in the car and lock the door," she shouted over the sound of the engine.

"Do you have to leave me alone?" I shouted, but I knew she couldn't hear.

I stood up and tried to freeze my face muscles into the right pose: brave. Hope looked at me then and silently mouthed the words: *I love you.* She hadn't said that to me since I couldn't remember, so I was glad that Michael slammed the cycle into gear and they roared off.

The sound of the engine sailed around in my ears as dust slowly settled on the road again. The taillights left an echo of their path the way a sparkler does on the Fourth of July. And my sister, my only sister in the world, had just told me she loved me.

Yet part of me felt like a little kid left all alone again, and I could feel the sludge of self-pity start to suck at me.

I picked up a rock and threw it as far into the barren landscape as I could. Stranded. How could she leave me alone? She had to, of course, but still . . . This mess was of my own doing, anyway. *Come on, Carin. Straighten up.* What use was self-pity when no one was around to whine to? I picked up three more rocks and threw them with all my might and hollered the biggest shout I could shout. It felt great.

I walked over to the car and looked west. A last long stripe of orange hugged the edge of the Earth, like a big wide lip. It was the sun's good-bye kiss for today. "Good-bye, Sun," I yelled stupidly, and waved. Sometimes you do things when you're alone that you'd never do if anyone were around.

The air was already cooling off; I stepped out of my dress and into the warm car. With the doors locked, and the windows up most of the way, I had nothing to do but watch the land and sky grow darker and darker. There was a faint alpenglow over the mountains, the very end of the sunset. I tried to stay calm. It was already nine. So much for Hope's interview. I took a deep breath.

What I knew I needed to do was *not* to think about a herd of tarantulas marching over the foothills toward me. Ditto for scorpions. I also knew I shouldn't think about a UFO stopping by and deciding I would be a good life-form to kidnap. Lastly I knew I shouldn't think about snakes climbing up the car and slithering in through the window—I rolled the windows to the top—or gliding up inside the air conditioner vent or some other car part I didn't know the name of.

I tapped my foot and began to hum. When you know you have things you don't want to be thinking about, tapping and humming can be a big help. I added finger snapping, and all of these things were helping me focus, focus, focus.

19

Humming, tapping, snapping. I was doing pretty well keeping my mind away from all the things I didn't want to think about until someone tapped on the window, and I let out a bloodcurdling scream.

Fortunately, it was Hope.

"What happened?"

I unlocked her door and she slid in, panting.

"Is everything okay?"

"I ran," she said, which I didn't think was a very complete answer.

"What happened? Michael—?"

She took two last long breaths and sat very straight. "After a couple hills, I thought how dumb this was"—she panted again. "I hated leaving you, so I asked him to stop"—one more pant—"and let me off. He's taking the money to the gas station. He knows the guys and he said when they get a free truck, they'll come for us."

"Are you sure? What if he—?"

"I'm sure. He's no creep." She had a sheepish grin on her face that nearly glowed in the dark.

"Hope?"

"He gave me his number and asked me to call him."

"A date?!"

Hope nodded, and I laughed. "So don't go telling everybody how desperate your big sis is to get a date."

"Like running out of gas in the middle of Nowhere Land?"

"Yeah."

"Except it wasn't you who ran out of gas, Hope. It was me. Why did you say it was you?"

She shrugged. "You might have been driving, but hey. Besides, have you forgotten you don't have a license?" She slipped into a slow western drawl. "What if he'd been the sheriff in these here parts?"

"I'm glad you're back. You know how it is when you're alone, trying to keep the creepies away."

She put her arm around my neck and pulled my head close. "I know exactly how it is."

We leaned back in our seats and looked into the sky. More and more stars joined the early ones, as if they were part of a floor show and it was their time to go on. "Man, there's nothing like this anywhere, is there? I mean, you have to be out in the country, somewhere close to Reno, Nevada, to see all these stars on this exact night."

"Yeah."

"This is the closing scene in our trip."

"Almost. Except for Dad's? And"—I could hardly say the words—"your interview."

Hope leaned toward the clock. "It's quarter past nine. I might make it. At least I did my nails." She sat up straight.

"I think I should do my hair up in something cute, no, something stylish—but not too stylish, in case her style is different from mine. But I need to look like I'm fresh out of Chicago, you know?"

"Hope, you definitely look like you're fresh from Style-Land."

"Serious?"

"Believe me, yes."

We babbled on, each of us probably hoping that our chitchat was stalling the clock, forcing each minute to drag by more slowly, even by a few seconds. Hope fixed her hair in the darkness, which she thought was a hopeless thing to do.

"Hope, I have to tell you. It might be better than in the light."

She burst out laughing. "You rascal."

We both heard an engine at the same time and saw lights bobbing over the foothills in front of us. The small truck stopped across the road and we were out of the car in a flash. In a few minutes, our tank had a little gas in it, and we were on our way to Joe's gas station for more. Moving again—finally.

20

Before long, we were winding our way into Reno, hooking onto the interstate, passing the exits we didn't want and gliding off on the one we did. The road seemed to glow under the silvery streetlights.

Hope said in a dreamy voice, "Can you believe how far we've come?"

Her words dangled in the air like the sound of my mother's clocks in the kitchen in Davenport. We both seemed to be thinking about how far we'd come in so many ways. I felt more grateful for my sister than I ever had before. "Yes," I answered. "Far."

She glanced at me, and we smiled at each other the way best friends smile at each other.

She flicked her nail on the car clock. "Look. Twenty-five to ten. I'm going to make that interview. A cinch, right?"

I laughed. "For you? Yeah, cinch-y."

She pulled onto Dad's street and into the driveway. The headlights lit up a wide banner taped across the garage door that read: WELCOME MY BEAUTIFUL SWEET-HEARTS.

"Do you think he was expecting us?" Hope said with a laugh.

We looked at each other and clasped hands for a second, a good solid second.

Light sprayed across the lawn as the front door opened. Dad stood there with a big grin and wide-open arms.

Hope and I jumped out of the car and, together, ran to him.